Not in
THE PLANS

NOT IN THE PLANS

EMILY SILVER

To Tina Snider and Johnnie Walker without whom this book would not exist!

And Claire…thank you for your help on all things British hockey <3

Chapter One

OLIVIA

"Oh, no. No, no, no."

That *has* to be wrong. My manager told me the filing deadline to get the Welsh player was next week. As in, five days from now. I was getting it done early so we wouldn't have any issue.

Now the portal isn't loading. Refreshing the screen, I'm now greeted with another message.

Trade deadline has passed.

I'm going to be sick. I still have time according to my manager, but no. No matter where I click on the screen, the same message appears.

Trade deadline has passed.

How in the world am I going to explain this tomorrow?

It's after six, meaning I'm one of the last few people in the office. Popping up from my desk chair, I stick my head out the door. All the lights are dim.

I take that back. I'm the only person that is still here.

Meaning my mess-up can't be dealt with tonight.

I've come to realize this is one of the many nuisances of working for the Elite Ice Hockey League in London.

Having just graduated from university with a business degree, this was one of the first job offers I received. Even though I knew next to nothing about ice hockey, I accepted the position.

I work hard and am one of the few people that always stays late to finish my work. Maybe if I'd left early like everyone else, I wouldn't even know about this issue and could deal with this tomorrow.

"What am I going to do?" I groan, dropping down into my desk chair. "Think, Olivia, think."

If I email my manager, maybe they can make a quick call to get this whole mess sorted. Or, it could mean that I get fired that much sooner.

Great. There's another thought that flits through my head. There is no way I botch this up and keep my job.

I shove my hands through the soft curls of my light brown hair, but am met with resistance from the tight bun it's in. A headache gathers between my eyes.

How could I have missed something so simple? I click back over to my email to see where the deadline email sits with a bright red flag.

Five days from now.

How in the world is it already closed then?

Bile rises in my throat. I can't lose this job. It's not like I'd have anywhere to go if I lost it. My phone buzzes from its cradle next to my keyboard.

IMOGEN

Livvy, you must come drink with us this evening

SIENNA

Meaning, please come keep us in line

SIENNA

Imogen has already had one too many cocktails and is looking like she wants to take the bartender home

IMOGEN

No I don't!

IMOGEN

It's the man sitting in the corner of the bar I want to take home

SIENNA

Same difference, love

IMOGEN

Livvvvvvy! Pleaseeeee!

GRABBING MY PHONE, I tap away an immediate answer at my two best girlfriends.

OLIVIA

Considering today might be my last day at work, you two are buying and will have to keep me in line for once

THAT GETS ME AN IMMEDIATE RESPONSE.

IMOGEN

You're losing your job?

SIENNA

What happened?

IMOGEN

You're like the best employee they have

SIENNA

Seriously, we never see you

IMOGEN

We're at the usual pub

SIENNA

Get a cab

SIENNA

We'll see you soon

WELL, if I am not going to have a job tomorrow, I might as well get pissed.

"LIV! YOU CAME!" Imogen shouts, staggering toward me.

"How much have you had to drink?" I wrap my arms around her waist so she doesn't tumble into a nearby table.

"Only a few fingers of bourbon."

"And some shots," Sienna points out as I steer us back to the table.

"It's a Thursday night. I'm allowed to drink."

"Don't you have work in the morning?" I ask, dropping into the empty seat next to her.

"Today is my Friday. No work for me."

"Ahh. Well, that makes two of us."

Sienna snaps for the passing waiter and orders me my usual glass of gin and ginger beer. Nothing fancy or over-the-top for me.

"Please tell us what happened."

Sienna brushes her perfectly sleek, dark auburn hair over her shoulder. She is never *not* perfectly made up.

The same for Imogen, even if her blue eyes are glassy. Her blonde hair is pulled back into a low bun, secured at the nape of her neck, not a hair out of place.

My best friends are stunners.

"I missed filing the paperwork for the preseason trade deadline, and now I'll be lucky to have a job tomorrow."

"Wait, I thought that was next week. You've been talking about it for the last month, it seems," Sienna says.

"No, I haven't."

I smile at the waiter as my drink is dropped off. I take a gulp, needing it to cool everything that is floating inside me. The juniper taste explodes on my taste buds.

Imogen rolls her eyes at me. "Yes, you have. You've been using it as an excuse for not coming out even though it's a few clicks of a mouse."

"See? Even we know what your job entails," Sienna confirms. "Pretty sorry excuse to blow off your best friends."

"I'm not blowing you off," I huff. "I'm busy. I have work."

"We all do, love. You make a point to stay busier than the rest of us."

"Nothing wrong with wanting to do a good job." My voice is indignant as I settle back in the uncomfortable high-top chair.

This is why I don't like coming to these places. Limited seating, overpriced drinks, and too many people.

"You need to let your hair down and live a little," Imogen tells me. Her hand grabs the clip holding my brown hair in place and lets it flow around my shoulders.

"That wasn't necessary." I grab the hair accessory from her and clasp it around my purse strap.

My very favorite Mulberry bag. The forest green, pebbled leather purse with the gold clasp was my treat to myself when I got this job.

The very same one I might be losing tomorrow.

"Okay, let's say you do lose your job. Maybe tonight you do something out of the ordinary."

"What would be out of the ordinary for me?"

"Anything," Imogen says.

"Well, that's quite rude," I fire back, sipping on my drink.

Sienna waves her off. "Ignore her. She hasn't had sex in a month, and it's doing things to her head."

I nearly spit out my drink. "Sienna! You cannot say things like that."

"It's true," Imogen confirms.

"Nothing wrong with that." A gleeful smile spreads across Sienna's face. "That's what you need to do."

"Yes!" Imogen claps her hands. "Liv, we need to find you a man to take home this evening."

This time, I do spit my drink out in the most unladylike of ways. "I am not taking a man home."

"There are plenty of men in here that would be perfect for her." Sienna ignores my protestation.

"Yes. I think a buttoned-up guy would be more her type." Imogen points to a group of men with briefcases at their feet. "They look like nice barristers. She could probably get a decent night out of one of them."

"Excuse me. I am sitting right here."

"And?" Imogen flags down our server and orders another drink. I order a second round for myself with a water. "Honey, we love you, but you do need to live a little."

Sienna nods. "You do."

"Why am I friends with you two?" I groan.

"Because you love us back," Sienna confirms.

"Some days, but I do not know why."

"I know why." Imogen pokes me in the side. "Because the guy I'm eyeing has someone with him that is eyeing you."

"What?"

There is no way that anyone would be eyeing me over my two friends. I'm about as plain as it gets.

With plain brown hair, blue eyes, a few freckles, and a small gap between my front teeth, I don't think most men look twice at me.

Nothing I'm not used to, since I grew up hearing how ordinary I look.

"He is *sexy*," Sienna says. "He is eyeing you like you're a snack."

"He is not," I hiss, slapping her hand away.

"Olivia. If you do not go say hi to that man, I will never speak to you again."

Imogen halts the conversation as our drinks are replenished. I glug down a few sips of water before finishing my first drink. I'm not drunk, but just on the right side of buzzing. Two glasses is my max. I never go above that. I don't like being a sloppy drunk.

It's those few sips that have curiosity licking at my brain. "You're not joking? There is someone checking me out?"

Sienna's grin seems to take up her entire face. "Yes. At the bar over your left shoulder. With the brown hair."

Trying my best to play coy, I spin in my seat, acting as if I'm searching for our server. It doesn't take more than a moment until I spot the man they're talking about.

A smile plays on his lips. His hair is a thick, dark brown

mess with grey at the temples, like he's been running his hand through it. Scruff lines his jaw. The corners of his eyes crinkle as he holds his glass up to me.

"You weren't kidding." I nearly come off the seat as I turn back to my friends. "Why is someone that hot looking at me?"

"Because you are gorgeous, babe," Imogen tells me. "Do you want me to go talk to his friend so we can break the ice?"

Nerves burble up in my stomach. I have never been the forward one. Never one to make the first move.

"No," I snap. The last thing I want is for this man—this sexy, god of a man—to think I can't speak to him.

"Does that mean you're going to go over and talk to him?"

I nod, taking one last fortifying sip of gin.

"Yes." I point between the two of them as I sling my bag over my shoulder. "And just because I'm speaking to this man—"

"A very sexy man," Sienna interjects.

I ignore her. "Does not mean I am going home with him."

"We'll see about that." Imogen waggles her perfectly waxed brows at me.

Spinning on my heel, I head towards the bar.

Towards the sexiest man I've ever laid eyes on.

He tracks me as I approach him. The nerves turn to flames. I want to throw myself at him as I stop in front of his seat.

But I don't. I do the sensible thing instead.

"Hello."

Chapter Two

TAG

Fuck me. I don't know if I've ever been so tired in my whole damn life. And that's saying something since I played hockey.

Jet lag is a bitch.

Having arrived early yesterday morning in London, I've been powering through exhaustion. With a new job starting in a few days, I wanted to acclimate to the time difference.

Even on my second day here, I can barely keep my eyes open. They're as dry as sandpaper.

Scrubbing a hand down my face, I take in my small apartment. Flat, as I was reminded several times by the cabbie that dropped me off.

Flat. I need to remember that. I've already gotten several weird looks when I went to the corner store to grab groceries so I don't starve.

Thankfully this place is already furnished, so I don't have to mess around with finding furniture for it.

The entirety of this *flat* could fit into my bedroom back home. The kitchen is small, with a wall that cuts through the living room. There's a sliding door across from the kitchen that leads to the bedroom and bathroom.

At least there's a decent view of a park across the way. Better than the graffitied brick on the other side of my building.

Nothing fancy, but since I don't need much, it's fine. I'm only here on a short-term contract with the Lightning. I have a lot to do in the way of proving myself to the team.

My phone buzzes in my pocket.

ALFIE

Did you make it okay?

I SMILE down at the message from my new assistant coach. I've called and texted with him a few times since I got the offer. Coming in during the middle of the season is never a good thing. The team was floundering with their old coach, and the owner of the team wanted to mix things up.

TAG

I did

Fucking tired as hell, but I made it

You know what they say beats jet lag?

What?

A pint at the pub

I BURST OUT LAUGHING, dropping onto the couch that is entirely too small for my six-four frame. Maybe I will need to find some new furniture.

Is that so?

Especially if the assistant coach is buying

How can I say no to that?

Great. See you in twenty

I PUNCH the name of the pub into my phone and see that it's a short walk away. This is something I'm not used to. At home in Nashville, I had to drive everywhere. Now, with a card for the subway loaded onto my phone, I don't need a car.

Stepping into my black boots, I head out into the London night.

Cars are rattling along the road. Something else I need to get used to—driving on the other side of the road.

I didn't do much traveling growing up. With hockey, it took precedence over everything. I never experienced anything like this.

An Indian restaurant is next to a laundromat which is next to a cell phone repair store. Down the way is where I stopped in for food. And beyond that is a small park before a music store.

An eclectic mix of everything.

Something I'm already finding in my neighborhood? There is no shortage of pubs. Every façade seems to want to one-up the other. Colors explode out of hanging flower baskets. Large windows are open to tables with stools, people crowded around with beers in hand.

Finding the pub Alfie mentioned, I squeeze in through a group of well-dressed people and scan the crowd. I've only seen Alfie in pictures, but I spot him immediately.

With curly red hair and glasses, he stands out. I never would have thought this man to be a hockey player, but he was one of the best to ever play for the Lightning. He was brought on as a new assistant coach.

They cleaned house when they let go of the old coach.

"Alfie."

"Stanley. Good to finally meet you in person."

I shake his proffered hand.

"Please, call me Tag."

"Still weird to me they hired an American." He flags down the bartender. "What'll ya be having?"

"IPA if you have one."

"Got it." The bartender nods and grabs a glass to pull my drink. "Cheers, mate."

I smile at him as I raise my glass in toast. "I think I'm going to like it here."

I sip on the hoppy beer, letting it buzz through my veins. Now that I'm out, I feel better. More awake.

"How's the flat?" Alfie asks. "Everything good there?"

I waggle my head in a figure eight motion. "Fine. Might need a new couch though. Not made for an ex-hockey player."

"Definitely not. I've got a place I can recommend for you."

"Thanks."

My eyes scan the crowd and I'm drawn to the trio of women laughing at the high-top table across the bar, especially one in particular.

She is the definition of prim and proper. A white

blouse, fastened to her neck. Black blazer. Skirt that hits just above the knee and low heels. Brown hair tumbles around her shoulders.

What I wouldn't do to ruffle that woman up.

"You still with me?" Fingers snap in front of me. A huge grin is on his face.

"What? Sorry."

"I take it you're single then, mate?"

"I am."

For the first time in a long time, saying that doesn't hurt. Having gotten divorced last year, it doesn't stir up all sorts of feelings to tell him that.

It feels like this is a fresh start.

"Are you looking for anything?"

"Why do you say that?" I sip my drink.

"You were being quite obvious," Alfie tells me.

"Was I?" I laugh. "It's been a minute since I've dated anyone."

"You need tips? You could always order her and her friends a round."

I spin on my stool to face my new coworker. "I'm good. If she comes over, I'll take it as a sign."

"You sure?" he asks.

I quirk a brow at him. "Do you want to go talk to them? Do *you* need tips?"

"Fuck off." Alfie flips me off. "Is this what I have to look forward to? You being a cheeky shit?"

"You'll learn to love me."

"If you can turn the Lightning around, I will. Christ, we're terrible," he tells me.

"I think we have a good team."

"Aren't you an optimist?"

I watched footage of the team before I got here. We certainly aren't the best team in the league, but not the worst. There's a lot of work to be done and I'm excited for it.

"So I've been told."

"You got that right." Alfie nods behind me before standing and making himself scarce.

"What?"

Before I know what's happening, the sexy woman from earlier is standing in front of me. She's a solid foot shorter than I am.

A smile plays on her lips. "Hello."

God, is her accent ever adorable. It matches her perfectly. Prim and proper. Posh, if you will.

"Hi there."

Her eyes go wide. "American?"

I nod. "Just arrived in town yesterday."

"What brings you to England?" she asks.

"New job."

"Well, welcome to London. Hopefully you'll find it amenable."

"Amenable?" I lean back in my barstool and wave a hand for her to take Alfie's vacated seat. "So far I'm finding it very *amenable*."

She fights a smile as she hops onto the chair, crossing her legs at her ankles.

"What's your name?" she asks.

"Tag. You?"

"Olivia."

"Olivia. Well, it's very nice to meet you." I hold out my hand for her to shake. She studies it before taking it.

Damn, is her skin ever soft. I can't help but rub my thumb over the back of it. Her fingernails are painted a soft pink. I shouldn't be noticing these things about her. I'm here to focus on hockey, not women.

"You too." She gives me a shy smile. "Do you live in this area?"

I nod. "A short walk. Still need to get my bearings, but I find I like this pub already."

"Oh yeah?"

"Quite the clientele here."

"I see."

A blush creeps up her cheeks. This is not how I expected the night to go. A pint with Alfie? Yes. Hoping to take this woman home? No.

Olivia sets her empty glass down on the bar and smiles at me. "What are you most excited to see here?"

I lean closer. "I don't want to talk about the sights."

"What do you want to talk about then?" she asks, sipping from a lowball glass, nearly empty with clear liquid.

"You."

"M-me?" she stutters. "Why me?"

"You came over here to talk to me. You can't only want to talk about London."

"You're right, I don't."

"Then what do you want to talk about?" I ask her.

This close, there's a fire in her blue eyes. "Well, I did come over here for a reason."

"And that reason is?"

"Ask me to go home with you, Tag."

The corner of my mouth pulls up in a smile. There is something damn sexy about how this woman says my name. I've never heard it sound so sweet.

"Is there a reason you can't ask me, Olivia?"

"Because a lady never propositions a man."

Gulping down one last sip of my beer, I set my drink down. "Is that so?"

She nods. "Your clock is ticking."

"Well, then, Olivia. Would you like to go home with me?"

"Where do you live?"

"What?" Her about-face throws me for a loop.

"Where do you live? I need to tell my friends where I'll be."

"Safety first. I appreciate that." Grabbing a cocktail napkin, I flag the bartender down to pay my bill and pull out my phone for my address—something I need to memorize. "Here you go."

She takes it from me, finishing her drink. "Be right back."

Olivia rushes by in a whiff of roses and gin. Fuck. She smells delicious. I want that smell all over my bed. All over me. Fuck. It has my cock stirring in my pants as I watch the woman who has captured my attention rush back to her friends.

They glance over at me as I give them a little wave.

This was not how I intended to spend my second night in London. I planned on going to bed at a reasonable hour so I could sleep off the jet lag before heading to the rink to get to know my new team. Now? Jet lag is nowhere in sight.

That plan is now out the window as Olivia strides over to me, purse secured to her shoulder.

I stand, holding my hand out to her. "Do I have your permission to take you home now?"

"Yes."

Thank fuck.

She takes my hand and I lead her out of the pub.

"It's a short walk this way."

"Lead the way, Tag."

Chapter Three

TAG

"You want anything to drink?" I ask, shutting the door behind me.

"No, thank you." Olivia spins, shedding her blazer and purse. "I'm good."

"No second thoughts?" I ask.

Now that we're away from the bar, from the haze of alcohol, I want to make sure she still wants this as much as I do.

Because fuck, this woman is sexy as hell, and I can't wait to peel her out of this buttoned-up outfit she's wearing.

"No." She shakes her head.

"Good. Do—"

I can't even finish my question before she throws herself into my arms and attacks my mouth with hers.

Cupping her cheek, I slow her motions and take control.

Olivia's skin is soft. Smooth. Walking us back into the wall, I heft her into my arms. I swallow each moan and whimper as my tongue connects with hers. As I explore this sweet mouth that tastes like gin and ginger.

I can't imagine how good it's going to be to discover every inch of this woman's body.

"Tag," Olivia moans as I move my lips down her jaw.

"Good, baby?"

"Yes. Don't stop."

I lick down her neck, feeling her pulse throb. "I don't plan to. Not until I'm buried inside you and you're screaming my name."

Her fingernails dig into the back of my neck, urging me on. My dick is hard as a rock and dying to get inside her.

"Oh, please."

"Please?" I pull back, tucking a lock of brown hair behind her ear. "So polite."

"What can I say?" She smirks. "I was raised with good manners."

"Well then. I believe it's good manners to do everything I say." Dropping her to her feet, I take a step back and assess the woman in front of me.

From the blouse that hides everything to the skirt that clings to her hips. Her hair? Well, I can't wait to make a mess of it.

To strip her of this well-mannered façade. To see her taking my cock and coming all over it.

"Then what should I do first?"

Exactly the question I wanted to hear. I rub my hand over the denim that's caging in my dick.

"Lose the blouse."

Deft fingers undo each button, revealing more and more of her pale skin. When she pulls it from the hem of her skirt, I have to fight the urge to take her right here.

A pale pink bra encases her small breasts. Even from

here in the dim lights of my apartment, I can see her tight nipples.

I am going to have so much fun devouring them.

"What next?" Olivia throws her shirt at me.

"Skirt."

Kicking off her heels, she reaches behind her to unfasten the zipper. It echoes in the small space. Or maybe that's the blood rushing to my head because every inch of skin she reveals has me wanting her more and more.

Damn. Did I ever get lucky that I decided to go out tonight and spot this sexy woman.

With her standing in front of me in nothing but her bra and underwear, I close the distance between us.

"Do you know how sexy you are?" I circle her, crowding her from behind and letting her feel what she does to me.

"Why don't you tell me?"

"Mmm." I press my lips to the spot where her neck and shoulder meet. "So soft. So sweet."

I drag my calloused palms up her arms and pull her into me. Brushing her hair to the side, I unclasp her bra and let it fall to the floor.

My hand finds her stomach and I squeeze her to me.

"These curves? Fuck, Olivia. I can't wait to hold on to them as I pound into you. To see how perfect you are at taking all of me. To taste every inch of you."

"Stop tormenting me then and do it."

I nip at her neck. "What's the magic word?"

She purrs. "Please."

Scooping her into my arms, I carry her into my room and toss her into the middle of the bed. Grabbing the neck of my shirt, I pull it off and throw it into the corner next to my suitcases. I've barely had time to unpack since getting here.

I cover her body with mine, capturing her mouth in a heated kiss. I suck on her greedy tongue as my hands roam over her soft skin.

By the time I'm done with her, every inch of her skin will be marked as my own.

Licking and sucking my way down, I press gentle kisses to each breast before playing with her nipples, laving each one with attention.

Olivia's soft moans hit my ears, and I love hearing what I do to her. The way she starts to writhe underneath me. My hand slides down her stomach to find the band of her underwear.

I dip my fingers below to find her already wet.

"How long have you been like this, baby?"

I can't help the nickname that slips out.

"Since I walked into your flat."

"Well then, I think it's time to see this sweet little pussy of yours."

Giving her a devilish smile, I pull her cotton underwear off and settle between her now spread legs.

The small patch of hair there is perfectly trimmed.

"What do you want me to do now, Tag?" Olivia asks.

I love the way she says my name. Prim and proper, laced with want.

Throwing her legs over my shoulders, I nip at the tender skin of her inner thigh. "I want you to lie here while I eat you out. You're going to come on my tongue before I fuck you senseless."

"Oh, please. Do that." I peer up at her, and her blue eyes focus on mine before I capture her clit with my lips. "Oh!"

Olivia slides her fingers into my hair, gripping tight to the point of pain.

I fucking love it. I continue my ministrations on her clit as I slip a finger inside of her.

"More. Please, I need more."

I don't think she knows what she's saying as she grinds down on my face. Her wetness coats my mouth as I work a second finger inside of her.

"God, your pussy is so tight. I can't wait to feel it squeezing me when you come."

"Gah!"

Her hand leaves my hair, sinking into her own. Goose bumps break out all over her skin as her pussy starts to strangle my fingers. She's close. I'm grinding down into the bed, trying to stave off my own release.

I'm not coming until I'm deep inside this woman.

"C'mon, Olivia. I want to taste you. Give it to me."

"Tag, I—"

She explodes on a shout. I lap up every single drop. Her legs squeeze my head as she rides my mouth through her orgasm.

"Delicious." I wipe my mouth. "Fucking delicious, baby."

Olivia is sated, eyes closed and body flush as I rock back onto my knees. I drag a lone finger up her leg, getting her attention.

Hazy, lust-filled eyes stare up at me. I don't know if I've ever seen someone look so beautiful before.

"You ready for my cock?"

Hopping off the bed, I strip off the rest of my clothes. My dick pops out, precum leaking from the tip.

"Oh my God. You're huge."

I smirk back at her, stroking my dick. My apparently *huge* dick. God, I like this woman. She doesn't filter her thoughts and tells you exactly what she's thinking. Olivia's face gives her away as she licks her lips.

"We'll go slow."

"How do you want me?" She sits up, eyes not straying from where I'm stroking myself.

"On your hands and knees."

She hurries to obey as I grab a condom from my discarded wallet and make quick work of rolling it down my hard length.

Situating myself behind her, I slide my dick through her wet folds.

Olivia turns, looking back at me. "What are you waiting for?"

Sweeping her hair off her back, I slowly push inside of her as I take her mouth in a heated kiss.

I swallow her gasps and moans as I sink into her tight, wet heat.

"That's it, baby. You're doing so good." I reach around and strum her clit. "So good, baby."

When I'm fully inside her, I let my hands trace circles on her back to let her adjust to my size.

I know I'm well-endowed, and even with one orgasm under her belt, I don't want to hurt this woman. Not if I plan on doing this again. And again.

All this pale, smooth skin is making it hard to focus on not erupting right now. I squeeze her ass, letting my fingers play with her crease.

"Have you ever been fucked here?" A few hours with this woman and a carnal, possessive need has taken hold over me.

I press my thumb to the tight pucker of her ass.

"No." She shakes her head as she presses her hips back against me. Oh yeah, she's adjusting nicely.

I lean over her. "Would you want that?"

It takes her a minute to answer. "Yes."

I rub my thumb over her one last time before pulling

away. "Maybe later. You're going to come all over my cock now."

"Then make me," she says.

Giving her ass one hard slap, I start to move. Gentle at first before going harder. Faster.

"You're driving me wild, Olivia. Your pussy is heaven." Sweat clings to my brow as I hold on to her hips.

"Tag. More. More."

Her pussy is squeezing my cock to within an inch of his life. My body is on fire. A rubber band ready to snap if I don't come. My balls are drawing up tight, but I'm not coming until she does.

My hips snap. The sound of skin slapping against skin echoes around the room. "Fuck! C'mon, Liv."

It doesn't take more than a few more thrusts before she's coming undone. It has me pumping harder. Her shouts bounce around in my head before I explode, emptying my release into the condom.

"Yes!"

I hold on tight as I pour everything inside her. Electricity bounces between the two of us as I still.

Holy fuck. I don't think I've ever come so hard in my life. My muscles are wrung out as I collapse on top of Olivia.

"That was incredible."

Slipping out of her, I tie off the condom and pull her into my arms. "Damn right it was."

She links her fingers with mine and snuggles into my hold. "Think you can do that again?"

I shift so I can look down at her. A playful smile sits on her face. "Are you questioning my abilities?"

"Never."

"Good. Because I plan on doing it all night long."

BUTLERS WHARF

Chapter Four

OLIVIA

Why is there light waking me up? Did I not shut the lights off last night? Or forget to close the curtains? Shifting to try and find the source of what's waking me up, I'm met with a hard body.

Oh my God.

Tag.

One arm is thrown over his eyes, another resting on his abs. The sheet covering him leaves very little to the imagination.

I still can't believe I did this. I don't regret it for one second. The number of times this man made me come is more than I ever have in my life.

The men before him were adequate at best.

Tag? He is on a whole different level. Not that it's one I can keep up. I don't do this, and now that the cold light of day is seeping in through the window, I need to leave and get back to real life.

A man like Tag is *not* real life.

Real life is facing the consequences of my actions at work.

Slipping out of bed, I cover myself with a stray pillow and shuffle into the kitchen to grab my skirt and blouse. My bra is lying on top of the pile.

"Crap. Where are my panties?"

I get dressed as best I can before wandering back into the bedroom.

Tag stirs. Shit. The last thing I want is to have to talk to him this morning. This is a one-night thing only. Even if I'd like for him to make me come again and again.

I spot the soft pink cotton of my underwear and grab them before he can wake up and stop me from leaving.

Bolting from the room, I grab my heels, shove the offending clothing item into my Mulberry bag, and am out the door.

I glance at my phone as I quietly close the door behind me, and it's blowing up with messages. A light rain is falling as I hail a taxi to take me back to my place.

IMOGEN

Did you make it home safely?

SIENNA

Check in, Liv!

SIENNA

How was Tag?

IMOGEN

We need deets, Liv!

IMOGEN

Liiiivy!

IMOGEN

Where are you, darling?

SIENNA

Maybe she's still with him

IMOGEN

Nothing like morning sex

SIENNA

Sigh

SIENNA

Now I wish I got some last night

OLIVIA

Would you two quit talking?

IMOGEN

She's alive!

SIENNA

Blink twice if you need us to rescue you

SIENNA

Does that mean you're safe?

SIENNA

Your status is unclear

IMOGEN

Obviously she is safe

IMOGEN

And annoyed with us

You are correct

I have to get to work

IMOGEN

I thought you were getting fired

SIENNA

She doesn't know that yet

I'm almost home

<<selfie in cab>>

I will give you details later

IMOGEN

Yes!

IMOGEN

We want them all

I meant about my job

IMOGEN

And I meant about the man

He has a name

IMOGEN

Hopefully you were screaming it last night

SIENNA

Stop it

SIENNA

You're making her blush

Am not!

IMOGEN

You totally are

IMOGEN

But go to work

SIENNA

We'll see you later, Liv

SIENNA

It's going to be okay

I hope so

IMOGEN

At least you went out in style

Back to ignoring you now

I TAP my phone on the card reader before stuffing it into my purse. Rushing out the door, I head straight to my flat. I don't have much time to shower and change before work. I start my coffee pot as I take the fastest shower I've ever taken. I'm already running behind. Not being at home made me not have an alarm to wake up to.

By the time I finish getting ready, I'm only twenty minutes late. I'm thankful my flat is so close to the rink. Being late when I might get fired?

Not your best moment, Olivia.

Only a few people are buzzing around the front offices by the time I make it in. Our receptionist waves hello to me. I smile at her, ducking into my office. If I stay here all day, maybe no one will come looking to fire me.

The morning goes by in the blink of an eye. I ignore checking my email for trade deadline information. Blissful ignorance, right?

Except as I'm leaving for lunch, I run right into my manager, Joe.

"Olivia. The new coach arrived this morning and we have some last-minute forms for him to complete. Mind running them over to him to get signed?"

"Erm, okay."

"Everything alright?" he asks, looking confused.

"No, I'm fine, Joe. Nothing else that you need to discuss with me?"

So much for not pointing out my error. Although, I

don't know if I could sit and deal with the stress of waiting for the other shoe to drop.

He quirks a brow at me. "No. I appreciate you getting the trade paperwork ready. Willis is going to be a fine addition to the team."

"What? I tried to file it last night and it said the deadline had passed."

"I got an email this morning that there was a glitch with the portal, but it's working now."

I nod. "Right."

He smiles at me. "Hopefully it didn't cause you any undue stress."

"It's fine. I'll get that paperwork filed today."

"Great. Thanks for taking care of it, Olivia."

"That's alright." I wave him off even though it really wasn't alright—more like panic-inducing and causing a string of bad decisions, but I don't need to let my boss know that. Taking the stack of papers from him, I stand from my desk. "I'll take these down now."

"Thanks." He gives me a warm smile before turning on his heel to leave. "And hey, if he needs help with anything getting settled in the city, make sure he's taken care of."

"I will." I head down the hall toward the coaches' offices. My nerves are a jumbled mess inside of me.

I'd been preparing for the worst. I thought I would be unceremoniously fired and escorted from the building by security.

Instead, I'm heading into the coaches' offices to get paperwork signed. Not the worst way to be spending this morning.

"Hey, Olivia," Danica, the coaching assistant, greets me as I walk into the offices.

"Hi. I'm looking for"—I run my finger over the paperwork, looking for our new coach's name—"Stanley Easton."

"He's back in the office. You know the way."

"Thank you." I smile at her, heading between the shared workspace toward the back of the offices. I recognize a few people down here, am friendly with them, but I don't make a point to socialize with people from the office.

Finding the correct door, with a brand-new name placard on the front, I knock.

"Come in."

"Am I interrupting—" Peeking my head inside, my jaw hits the floor.

There is no way this is happening. There is no way that the man sitting in front of me is the man I went home with last night.

Tag.

My legs wobble. I cross the short distance in the small room and drop down into a vacant seat. I clutch the papers to my chest like they're the only lifeline I have.

I slept with our coach.

"Alfie, would you give us a minute?" His eyes stay locked on mine.

If only the ground would open me up and swallow me whole.

"Everything okay?" he asks.

"Perfectly fine."

I do my best to ignore the assistant coach as he gets up and leaves the office. I have no issue with him. It's the man that has a grin that would make the Cheshire cat proud.

"Well, isn't this a surprise." Tag leans back in his desk chair, crossing his arms over his chest.

His very well-defined, muscular chest. One that I spent the night exploring.

Don't go there, Olivia.

"You said your name was Tag!" I hiss. It's the first thing that comes to mind.

Is it possible to die of embarrassment? Because I think I'm about ready to take my last breath.

This is why I never do anything impulsive.

Sleeping with a man that I had one conversation with before I suggested we go back to his place? I never do that.

And he just so happens to be the new coach of the hockey team that employs both of us.

Maybe no one will talk about this in my eulogy.

Oh, who am I kidding? Imogen would love it.

Died of embarrassment after having a one-night stand with the hockey coach.

"I go by Tag. It's a nickname. Stanley is too stuffy for me."

I scoff. "You should have given your real name. I feel like you lied to get me to sleep with you."

Tag stands, coming around the desk to stand in front of me. The papers in my hand are still clutched tight to my chest. He drops his hands on the arms of my chair. When he leans in towards me, he is overwhelming.

The scent of his cologne.

The flex of his jaw.

His gaze staring down into mine.

Heat racks my body. No man has ever made me feel like this. Adequate, maybe, but not like I want him to devour me again.

"Make no mistake, Olivia. You approached me. You asked to come home with *me*. If you want to lie to yourself, by all means, go right ahead. But I know whose name you were screaming last night."

Warmth blooms in my cheeks. I should not be thinking about how he made me feel.

I have never felt so good in my life. So satisfied. If Tag

is half as good at coaching as he is at giving orgasms, I'd say the Lightning are going to turn things around.

"What are you thinking?" Tag grasps my chin and pulls my gaze back to his.

"I need you to sign these papers."

His eyes dart down toward my chest before looking back up. "That's what's causing this pretty little flush all over your face?"

I nod, doing my best to fight the reaction I'm having to him.

"Yes."

He grins. "I don't believe you."

I stand, pushing him out of my space. "I don't care if you believe me or not. I'm here for business purposes."

Tag leans back, resting his perfect arse against the edge of the desk.

"As opposed to last night."

"You can't say things like that," I whisper.

"Like I didn't think I'd see you again because you snuck out of my apartment like a thief in the night?"

"Flat," I correct.

That earns me a smirk. Tag—Stanley—is still hovering over me. I can't decide if I want to push him away or pull him closer.

All I know is, I need to get out of this cramped space before I do something stupid. I thrust the papers at his chest.

"Sign these."

I scurry out of his office like the coward that I am. I don't stop until I'm safely in my office with the door shut. The last thing I need is for anyone to come in here while I look like the cat that ate the canary.

Tag is our new head coach. The man I slept with. There is no way I'm going to be able to talk myself through this. Pulling out my phone, I message the two people who will.

OLIVIA

Free for dinner tonight?

SIENNA

I have a date tonight, sorry!

IMOGEN

I can meet

IMOGEN

Everything okay?

SIENNA

Did you get fired?

No

But the man I slept with last night is the new coach of the Lightning

IMOGEN

He is not! Omg! I cannot believe you slept with the coach

IMOGEN

How did you not know it was him?

Because I've never seen him before now!

SIENNA

Reservation for three at seven at The Ivy Asia. Don't be late

What happened to your date?

SIENNA

This is way more important

Chapter Five

TAG

"Why do you look so smug?" Alfie asks, coming back into my office, a whistle around his neck. Checking my watch, I realize practice is set to start in thirty minutes.

"Do I?"

"Does it have anything to do with the woman that stopped by earlier?"

"Olivia?"

He nods. "She looks familiar."

"The girl from the bar," I supply.

Alfie whistles as I follow him out of the office toward the locker rooms. "Damn. You sure don't waste any time."

"I don't know what you're talking about."

I've never been one to kiss and tell, if you will. I never slept around before I got married. I was always a relationship guy. But there was something about Olivia I couldn't say no to.

Telling Alfie about her? It feels wrong.

Even if she slipped out before I was awake.

Finding out that she works here? That is a surprise. One I don't mind.

"You're really not going to tell me?"

"Nope." I shake my head as I open the door to the locker room. "Nothing to tell."

"Fine." Alfie eyes me before I shake him off.

The new defensive coach is waiting for us.

"Jack Jones." He holds his hand out in a no-nonsense manner.

"Stanley Easton. You can call me Tag."

"Alfie Hughes."

"Nice to meet you both."

His accent is thick, clearly English. Having done my research on him, I know he's an ex-hockey player. From what I gathered, he was happy staying in Europe to play. He was fucking talented as hell—could have made it in the NHL without a doubt. There was nothing I could find on why he didn't want to leave.

"I'm glad you're with us," I tell him. "We're going to need all the help we can get."

"Happy to be here." Jack gives me a clipped nod, dark brown hair peeking out from under his backwards baseball cap.

"You played for the Belfast Blades?" Alfie asks. "They're a great team."

"We were. Hopefully this team will be better."

That earns him a smile from me. "That's what I like to hear."

The guys are already gathered in the locker room, shooting the shit as they get ready for practice. It's not big by any means, but I know the European leagues don't have the same funds as the NHL.

Each guy has a folding chair in front of their stall.

Jerseys hang from hooks, and the smell of sweat and ice lingers in the air.

With not much room, the guys are crowded in one corner. This is one of the things that I missed the most when I retired from the game.

Having a good group of guys around you.

Our team wasn't the best. We had a coach that was putting in the time before he could retire. Making the play-offs? Never happened.

It didn't matter to me. I still love the sport.

And hopefully I can help turn this team around.

"Can I get everyone's attention?" I call out. The locker room quiets down as all eyes turn to me. "Stanley Easton. I'm your new coach. You can call me Coach or Tag. You'll find I'm easy to get along with, but I run a tight ship. If I say seven, I mean seven. Not five minutes later."

A few guys shift on their skates, looking nervous. They're the ones that are going to have the hardest time with me as coach.

"Jack and Alfie here are your new assistant coaches. If you have problems, I want you to come to one of us. I don't want things to linger or explode on the ice. That's not what I want this team to be about, you got it?"

"Yes, Coach," a few people say.

"Good. Now, let's hit the ice and get started."

I clap the guys on the shoulder as they file out past me. A few of the players I recognize from film, having studied last year's team before I started. They're talented. We have the skills to go far.

Guidance and training is what this team needs to turn things around.

"That was quite the welcome," Jack says from behind me.

"Don't want to scare them off just yet."

Grabbing my skates I left in here earlier, I lace them up and follow everyone out to the ice.

It's a smooth sheet of glass, a beacon calling me home. Breathing in the cold air, I know this was the right decision to move here.

After retiring a year and a half ago, I didn't have much of a plan. Throw in a divorce, and when the Lightning came calling, I jumped at the chance to coach a team.

Pushing off, I do a lap around the ice.

Scraping and scratching hits my ears as I sink into my skates. Muscle memory comes back, carrying me around the boards, as I get my feet under me.

Grabbing the whistle around my neck, I bring the metal to my lips. The sound echoes in the empty arena. It stops everyone where they are.

"Alright. I want to start with a little five-on-five. See where we are. We'll sub in, so let's split up and get going."

Jack and Alfie help to divide the teams as those not playing take their spots on the bench. Alfie drops the puck and the game starts.

There's talent for sure, but with that skill comes egos. One guy hogs the puck, allowing for an open man—and a potential shot on goal—to be missed.

Blowing the whistle, I change out the lines. It's more of the same. Selfishness seems to be the word of the day. A few guys manage to get some good passes in, but that's where it ends.

I wince, grabbing the whistle to change out the lines again. Damn. This is worse than I thought. Missed passes. Sloppy skating. Easy goals let in.

I've got my work cut out for me.

"Did you know they were this bad?" Jack whispers out of the side of his mouth.

"You don't clean house because they're good," I fire back.

After a few more changes, I blow my whistle and bring everyone to center ice. "That was a good first practice."

"We were crap, Coach," one of the guys shouts from the back.

Murmurs echo around me as they all agree.

"That's the last time I want to hear that." I look at each man standing in front of me. Some look dejected. Others tired. "I see strengths in each one of you. The lines you played on before might not be the same ones you'll play on this year. Jack, Alfie, and I are going to be mixing things up. We're going to run some drills, hit the weight room, and then hit the ground running tomorrow."

That earns me a few nods. I blow my whistle. "Good, now, suicides. Let's go."

I know we've got a long road ahead of us, but it's something I'm ready for.

"You're good at being diplomatic," Alfie tells me as we head back toward the offices once practice is over.

"Considering I was part of the worst team in the league for years, hearing 'you suck' isn't the way to earn their trust."

My time in Nashville wasn't great. I loved playing, but damn, we sucked. We were at the bottom of the league every season. My coach? He didn't care. It was a paycheck to him.

Once they got a new coach, things have been turning around for them.

I'm hoping the same can be said about the Lightning. I don't want to be kicked out after this season. Not after I've had such a *warm* welcome to London.

I shouldn't be thinking about Olivia again.

The very last place I expected to run into her was here. At my new job. But damn if I don't consider myself lucky.

The minx fled my apartment before I could get her number. Knowing now exactly where I can find her?

I have a feeling I'm going to enjoy this job more than I should.

Chapter Six

OLIVIA

Seven on the dot and I'm the only one here. I love my friends, but they are perpetually late. I've been waiting for ten minutes. I should know better, but I was always told growing up if you're on time, you're late. It's engrained into my DNA at this point.

I attempt to call my parents while I'm waiting, but I get no answer. Sighing, I leave a voicemail for my mum.

"Hi Mum, it's Liv. I wanted to see how you and Dad were doing. I haven't spoken to you in a few weeks. Hope you're doing well. Love you."

It's the most bland message to leave, but I doubt it'll get a follow-up. They ignored my message last month too.

As the time ticks past seven, I no longer wait for my friends. Giving the hostess Sienna's name, I follow her through the restaurant.

This is one of our favorite places in London. Pink flowers cover the ceiling and walls as we pass through the entryway. Blue and green glass floors are lit up from below. Oversized velvet booths fill the space as I'm led to a table in the corner overlooking the cathedral.

"Enjoy your evening."

"Thank you." I take the menu and set it down. I could recite it forwards and back.

Our server comes to the table and I order a drink while I wait.

"Sorry, babe. Sorry!" Sienna comes hurrying over, dropping a kiss on my cheek. "Tube was running behind."

I smile at her as she drops into her seat. It's always the tube running late with her.

"You know you didn't have to cancel your date," I tell Sienna as my usual drink is dropped off.

"And miss this? Never."

"I haven't missed anything, have I?" Imogen rushes towards us in a whirl of expensive perfume and a slinky black dress.

Stunning, as usual.

"No dish has been served," Sienna says.

"Good." Imogen rubs her hands together. "We'll get wine and then I want to hear all about your evening."

She waggles her brows at me, waving her hand at our passing server to order a bottle of red for the two of them.

"It is so embarrassing. I can't believe it happened," I groan, burying my face in my hands. "This is why I don't do things like this."

The bottle of wine is dropped off with two glasses. We wait as they're poured and handed to each of them.

"But the sex was good?" Sienna asks.

"How does that help the situation?" I hiss, gulping down half my drink. The gin helps to calm all my raging emotions.

Emotions I'm not used to feeling.

"But why are you embarrassed? You haven't told us that part," Imogen oh-so-helpfully points out.

"Because he's the new coach!" I bury my face in my hands.

"I'm still not seeing the problem," Imogen says. "You don't work under him. It's not a conflict of interest."

The noise of the restaurant grows louder in my ears. I can't believe I got myself into this situation. This is not what I was imagining would happen when I tossed all common sense out the window.

"C'mon, Liv. It's not the end of the world." Sienna's voice pulls me from my thoughts.

"No. In fact, this would be a wonderful chance to keep hooking up with him."

"What? I can't do that!" I shriek.

Imogen cackles. "Darling, you can. You're an adult and can do whatever you want. Including…wait, what's his full name?"

"Why?"

"Name." Sienna snaps her fingers at me. "Now."

"Stanley Easton III. Tag."

Imogen pulls out her phone and types away with a perfectly manicured finger. "Holy shit. I do not remember this man being this sexy last night."

Sienna's jaw drops and her eyes go wide as she stares at the image filling the screen. "Damn, Liv. I can't imagine how good the sex was."

Heat creeps up my cheeks. This is the last thing I need to be thinking about. How good things were with Tag.

Not just good. *Great.* God, it was the best sex of my life. I don't need to tell these two. I will never hear the end of it.

When the server comes back around, we order small plates to share for our dinner.

Dumplings. Bao buns. Spicy tuna rolls.

All of our favorites.

"It's okay, we know." Imogen winks. "Your face says it all."

"What? No, it doesn't." My hands fly to my cheeks, trying to hide the furious flush. I hate how my face gives me away.

"Give your poor sex-deprived friends all the details. We need them." Sienna clasps her hands under her chin. "Please?"

"Please, please, please," Imogen begs.

"Ugh, fine. It was incredible, alright?" I concede, dropping my voice to a low murmur to ensure no one around us hears. I don't want to flaunt my sex life to anyone else but these two. And even with them, they have to pry it out of me.

"I knew it." Imogen is preening. "I bet he made you come more than once."

"Multiple." I know it'll egg her on, but I do it anyway.

"If I didn't love you so much, I'd hate you," Imogen says. "I can't remember the last time I've had an orgasm without the use of a vibrator."

"You know there are apps for that, right?" Sienna asks.

"Weren't you telling us last week that you've had bad luck?" I ask.

"Maybe if there were Tags on these apps, I'd be more satisfied."

"Shush," Imogen quiets her. "The better question is, are you going to see him again?"

"I can't. It would be unprofessional of me to do so."

I know, before I even finish the sentence, the pushback I'm going to get from these two. I love them dearly, but they are so predictable.

"Why is it unprofessional?" Sienna asks, swirling her wine glass between her fingertips. "You don't report directly to him, do you?"

"No," I answer.

"And he doesn't report to you?" Imogen asks.

"No, of course he doesn't."

"Then what's the problem?" Imogen pierces me with her look that says she's calling me on my shit.

"Because he's not on my five-year plan!" I huff, throwing my arms in the air and narrowly missing the server and his tray. "Oh, I'm so sorry!"

"S'alright."

It seems whatever good sense I had, I left with Tag.

Dishes of steaming food are placed in front of us. My stomach rumbles, needing something to go with the gin I'm sipping on.

"Listen, Liv." Imogen starts grabbing small plates and passes them around as we each help ourselves to the appetizers. "I love you, darling, but to be honest, your five-year plan is boring."

"No, it's not. It's sensible," I scoff, smushing a bao bun between my fingers and taking a bite. Flavors explode on my tongue as I savor the ginger, pork, and kimchi.

Delicious.

"Find a nice guy. Get married. Have 2.5 kids. Get a dog. Buy a nice flat in the city." Imogen ticks each one off her fingers. "I get you want stability, but what's wrong with having some fun?"

"But it'll throw off my—"

"Your plan, yes. Make it a ten-year plan. Have something fun to think back on when you're old. Because this man?" Sienna nods towards Imogen's phone. "You want to have these memories."

A shirtless Tag fills the screen. What a shame I didn't get to lick all those abs of his.

Wait, what? Where did that thought come from?

"Look, Tag and I had fun, but that's it. It was a fun night. I need to focus on my plan."

"Make this man your five-minute plan. He is too sexy to leave that many orgasms on the table."

I choke around the bite I took, trying my best to swallow and suck down deep breaths.

"Imogen!" Sienna scolds. "Let's leave our poor friend alone. If she doesn't want to keep seeing Tag, then that's her decision."

I dab at the tears gathering in my eyes with my cloth napkin.

"I'm only saying she should have fun," Imogen defends.

I sip on my drink, letting my throat relax. "But…"

"Liv, let me ask you one question and then we'll put it to bed. Both of us." She eyes Imogen, who looks more frustrated than she should considering it's not her life in question.

"What's that?"

"Do me a favour. Try to think of a reason to say yes? Just one."

"Only one?" I mumble.

She nods.

"And you can't say because of the great sex. We already know this man can make you orgasm."

"Imogen!" I hiss. "You can't say these things in public."

She shrugs. Nothing bothers her.

But her point stands.

Every instinct is telling me the reasons to say no to starting things with this man.

He's not a part of my plan. The humiliation I would face at work if things went sideways is too much to bear. But…

"You don't have to tell us," Sienna starts, "but I can see the wheels spinning. Think about it, okay?"

"Okay."

The conversation moves to Sienna's date, but I focus on her request.

One reason to say yes?

Every voice in my head is shouting at me that Tag is not in the plans.

Say no, Liv.

They won't push the issue if you don't want to see this man again, but I will.

Like they said, what harm could come in having some fun?

From: Olivia Montrose <omontrose@londonlight-
ning.co.uk>
Sent: Thursday, August 14, 2025 2:16 PM
To: Stanley Easton III <seaston@londonlightning.co.uk>
Subject: Paperwork

Mr. Easton,

Kindly, please come to my office tomorrow at noon to finalise the rest of your paperwork for your visa. We will need your passport in order to do this.

Regards,

Olivia Montrose
Business Department
London Lightning

From: Stanley Easton III <seaston@londonlight-
ning.co.uk>
Sent: Thursday, August 14, 2025 2:18 PM
To: Olivia Montrose <omontrose@londonlightning.co.uk>
Subject: RE: Paperwork

Liv,

Are you always so formal in emails? It's cute. Kind of like the way you spell finalize with an s. I suppose one of the many things I have to get used to now that I'm in England.

Call me Tag.

From: Olivia Montrose <omontrose@londonlightning.co.uk>
Sent: Thursday, August 14, 2025 2:25 PM
To: Stanley Easton III <seaston@londonlightning.co.uk>
Subject: RE: Paperwork

Mr. Easton,

I would appreciate all communication to be done in a formal manner. Please don't be late tomorrow, as I have a full schedule.

Regards,

Olivia Montrose
Business Department
London Lightning

From: Stanley Easton III <seaston@londonlightning.co.uk>
Sent: Thursday, August 14, 2025 2:26 PM
To: Olivia Montrose <omontrose@londonlightning.co.uk>
Subject: RE: Paperwork

What's it gonna take for you to let your hair down, Liv? More drinks?

From: Olivia Montrose <omontrose@londonlightning.co.uk>
Sent: Thursday, August 14, 2025 2:47 PM
To: Stanley Easton III <seaston@londonlightning.co.uk>
Subject: RE: Paperwork

Tomorrow, noon. Do NOT be late, *Mr. Easton*.

PS – May I remind you that all emails require a signature line? Please be sure to update yours. I can assist you if you need help.

Olivia Montrose
Business Department
London Lightning

From: Stanley Easton III <seaston@londonlight-ning.co.uk>
Sent: Thursday, August 14, 2025 3:02 PM
To: Olivia Montrose <omontrose@londonlightning.co.uk>
Subject: RE: Paperwork

I'll take whatever assistance I can get. Maybe I can get some assistance in seeing the city. Showing me around my new home?

From: Olivia Montrose <omontrose@londonlight-ning.co.uk>
Sent: Thursday, August 14, 2025 3:08 PM
To: Stanley Easton III <seaston@londonlightning.co.uk>
Subject: RE: Paperwork

I can send you some local spots to visit.

Olivia Montrose
Business Department
London Lightning

From: Stanley Easton III <seaston@londonlight-ning.co.uk>
Sent: Thursday, August 14, 2025 3:16 PM
To: Olivia Montrose <omontrose@londonlightning.co.uk>

Subject: RE: Paperwork

Not the kind of assistance I want, Liv.

From: Olivia Montrose <omontrose@londonlight-
ning.co.uk>
Sent: Thursday, August 14, 2025 3:18 PM
To: Stanley Easton III <seaston@londonlightning.co.uk>
Subject: RE: Paperwork

Please see the attached reminder for the appropriate signature line instructions.

Olivia Montrose
Business Department
London Lightning

<<London Lightning Email Etiquette V2.3>>

Chapter Seven

TAG

"**K**nock, knock."

Pushing open the door, I find Olivia with her back to me, sitting at her desk, typing away. Her hair is pulled back into a complicated twist at the back of her head. Blue eyes are focused solely on her computer as she continues typing.

"I brought lunch to make this a more productive meeting."

"We need to get your paperwork done. We don't have time for lunch." She doesn't have to turn around to know it's me.

"Everyone has to eat at some point."

I head into her office, uninvited, and set down the brown paper sack on her desk.

"Tag." Her voice is wary. "I don't need lunch. We just need to finish your paperwork."

"I do." I drop into the seat across from her and take out my sandwich. "Gotta get my energy before practice."

Olivia spins in her chair, crossing her arms over her chest.

Do not think about how sexy she is.

It's the very last thing I need to be thinking about as I peel open the wrapper to my sandwich and take a hearty bite. I have no idea what it is, but I love it.

"Are you really going to sit here and eat in front of me?"

"No." I shake my head back and forth. "I was hoping you would eat with me."

Olivia studies me then the sandwich. It's like she's debating on whether taking the offer will involve something more with me.

"Liv, relax. It's a sandwich. I'm not asking you to go out with me."

"What? Why would you say that?" She looks stunned.

And it's fucking adorable.

"Because you seem to think this is more than lunch. It's a sandwich, Liv."

"Olivia," she corrects, but takes the sandwich. It's a small victory, but I'll take what I can get with her. Opening the Kraft paper, she peeks at what I ordered. "Coronation chicken?"

I shrug a shoulder. "Figured I'd try it. I have no idea what it is."

"It's chicken in a curry cream sauce. It's actually one of my favorites."

"Really? It's good."

"Guess you can be considered a Londoner now since you've tried it."

I shake my head. "I've got a long way to go before I consider myself a true Londoner. I haven't even seen Big Ben yet."

"You haven't?" That earns me a shocked look.

"Why are you surprised?" I question. "Jet lag kicked

my ass day one, and then I found myself enjoying more pleasurable activities on day two."

"Tag." A blush fills her cheeks.

Damn. I love that I can get a reaction out of this woman.

"I didn't say anything else." I take another bite, wiping my mouth with my napkin as the curry flavor bursts bright on my tongue. This small shop I found near the rink might become a new staple. Especially if it means I get more face time with Liv.

"You inferred it."

I take a bite of my sandwich, giving her a smug smile. Swallowing, I grab my water bottle and take a swig.

"Back to me being a Londoner. Do you have any tips on how I can become a *true* Londoner? I don't want to be stumbling around the city like an idiot."

Another smile from her.

"To start with, you've already been to the pubs."

"I have."

"I know the sights are probably cliché for someone like you, but you really do need to visit them at least once."

"Why would they be cliché for someone like me?" I ask, quirking a brow at her as I take the last bite of my sandwich.

"Well, I made the offer to our old coach and he laughed at me." Liv looks nervous, tucking a strand of hair behind her ear.

I know nothing about the old coach, but it makes me hate him. Who would ever turn down this woman, let alone be rude to her?

"I can assure you, Liv, that they are not cliché for me. I want to see everything London has to offer."

"Good." She looks pleased with herself. "I can arrange a private tour guide, if you would like."

"When are you free?"

"I didn't say me," she clarifies.

"What if I want it to be you though? You clearly know what you're talking about."

Leaning across the desk, Liv smiles at me. "You know who also knows what they're talking about? Tour guides."

"Touché."

"I'll put together something for you. You'll enjoy it."

"Okay." Crinkling the wrapper of my sandwich, I toss it into the empty bag. "I guess I'll take that. Think you could do something about the schedule so I can do it during the day?"

Liv laughs, and damn, if I don't want to spend the rest of my day sitting here doing it again. "I'm afraid if that were the case, then you wouldn't be a very good coach."

"Thus negating the entire reason the Lightning brought me here."

Wrapping up part of her sandwich, Liv tucks it away. "And seeing as how I like working for the Lightning, I wouldn't mind seeing the team start to win."

"I take it you're a big hockey fan then?"

Liv shrugs a shoulder. "I enjoy hockey, but I wouldn't say I'm a big fan."

I throw a dramatic hand over my heart. "You wound me. Not a big fan? That shouldn't be allowed when you work for a hockey team."

"I said I enjoy it." She points a finger in my face. "That's allowed."

"Okay. You enjoy hockey. What else do you enjoy?"

"Trying to learn more about me, Tag?" Liv quirks a brow at me.

"Sue me."

"I like things neat and orderly, Tag. I play the piano, I

like Jane Austen books and gin cocktails. What else would you like to know?"

She likes screaming my name, but I don't say that.

"And you like Coronation chicken."

"I do." She smiles. "What about you? What do you like?"

"I like hockey—"

"That's a given," she interrupts.

"Hockey," I continue. "Trying new things, no matter where I am, and my preferred beverage is beer."

"New things?" Liv asks. "Isn't that vague?"

"I tried Coronation chicken. I liked that. I want to do and see things in London, no matter how cliché they might be."

Liv rests her chin on her fist. "Say someone asked you to go skydiving, you'd do it?"

I nod. "Yes. Why not?"

She shudders. "No, thank you. I do not want to jump out of a perfectly decent airplane."

"You wouldn't try something just to say you did it? To face your fears?"

"Did you not hear where I said I like things neat and orderly, Tag? Jumping out of a plane would not be neat and orderly."

"Doesn't mean it wouldn't be fun to try."

"You are maddening." Liv says it with a smile. "If you think you're going to get me to jump out of a plane, you have another think coming."

I point a finger at her, having her right where I want her. "But I could get you to do other things?"

"Watch it."

Speaking of watch, I check mine and realize it's almost time for practice. "Time to hit the ice. Thanks for having lunch with me."

Liv goes back to typing on her computer. "You know, if you brought lunch again, I would be amenable to that."

Damn. That's practically a love confession from her. "That means I'm winning you over."

"I will see you around."

I wink at her before grabbing the trash and backing out. "Not if I see you first."

Chapter Eight

OLIVIA

"Mmm. Just like that."

"You like it?"

"Yes." I moan as a tongue slips inside my pussy. The way it curls? It's delicious. "More of that."

He obeys my command, devouring me. Licking. Sucking. Nipping at my clit.

"I'm so close."

Electricity zips through my veins as goose pimples erupt on my skin.

"C'mon, Liv. I want you to come on my tongue."

"Make me."

The demand in my voice sounds foreign to my own ears. I have never been the type to be overtly dominant in the bedroom. Submissive? Yes. But to tell my partner to make me come? Never.

"You're going to come on my tongue, Liv, then I am going to fuck this tight ass of yours so slow and sweet that you will be begging to come again."

"That would imply I've come a first time to be coming a second."

"Just you wait."

Calloused hands push my thighs farther apart, opening me up to his ministrations. Between that tongue and those fingers, this man is going to split me wide open.

"Oh, oh! Tag!"

Shooting out of bed, my entire body is a live wire as I wake from the most realistic dream I've quite possibly ever had.

"Oh my God."

Heat prickles my skin as the soft satin of my camisole rubs over my nipples. Peering into the mirror above the dresser, my face is bright red.

I had a sex dream.

About *Tag*.

This has never happened to me before. A sex dream? I'm better than this. I ignore the feeling sweeping through me as I hop out of bed and walk into the bathroom.

Flipping on the shower, I let the water heat up as I study my reflection.

I've dated men before. Having sex isn't a new thing for me. It's been satisfactory. Fine.

One night with Tag, and I've turned into a sex-crazed maniac.

Slipping out of my pyjamas, I step into the shower and let the hot water roll over me.

I mean, yes, I've never had someone give me that many orgasms in one night, but that doesn't mean I need to keep thinking about him.

Or dreaming about him.

Lathering my flannel, I scrub my body and…

Oh God.

I'm wet. Did I really come from a sex dream? I flip the water to cold, needing to cool off. This is too much for me.

The thought of seeing Tag at work has heat rushing

back into my face. Damn it. This day is not going to go well.

I finish my shower and get ready—pushing all thoughts and feelings about Tag from my mind.

Tag? Tag who? I don't need him.

I pull the buttons through the holes on my blouse before slipping into my blazer.

There.

Much better. Professional façade back in place. I can do this. Grabbing my bag, I sling it over my shoulder and leave for the office.

I blame it on having lunch with him the other day. That and Sienna challenging me to find one reason to say yes to, what, a fling with him? I mean, technically I said yes to lunch, right?

I shake my head as the arena comes into view.

I can hear Sienna scolding me in my head.

That's not what she meant and you know it.

That's the thing—it'd be too easy to say yes to Tag. To get lost in the sexy man and stray from my plan.

I don't need that.

No thinking of Tag or the way he made me come. *In a dream.*

Which is easier said than done.

Because the first person I run into at the rink is Tag.

"Better watch where you're going there, Liv."

"Mr. Easton. Hello."

A smile curls his lips. Sweat slicks his hair back. Athletic shorts cling to his strong, muscular thighs. The vest he's wearing is so tight, it shows off every one of his abs.

Do not think about him from your dream. Do not think about him *at all.*

"Feeling okay there?"

"What? Why wouldn't I be?" My hands fly to my cheeks. Will this flush be permanent? It seems whenever I think about this man, it crops up.

"You seem…flustered."

"I'm fine," I snap. "Just in a hurry to get to work."

"Sorry." Tag steps out of the way. "Maybe I'll see you for lunch."

His voice echoes in my ears as I hurry to the business department. The last thing I wanted was to bump into Tag.

My face is on fire as I scurry toward my office and slam the door shut behind me.

OLIVIA

Something happened to me that's never happened before

IMOGEN

What is it?

SIENNA

Are you okay?

I had a sex dream

SIENNA

You've never had a sex dream before?

IMOGEN

You've had sex, right :P

SIENNA

We know she has

IMOGEN

I was joking

IMOGEN

We all know she climbed the vast tree that is Tag

You two are not helping

SIENNA

There is nothing wrong with having a sex dream

Not when it's about Tag!

IMOGEN

I think that means you want to have sex with him again

I do not

SIENNA

Have you thought more about what I said?

Kind of?

I said yes to a sandwich

IMOGEN

Is that some weird sex thing?

It was a sandwich. An actual sandwich. The thing you eat?

SIENNA

Why are you stressing about said sex dream, Liv?

Because I work with the man! I can't be having sex dreams about someone I work with

IMOGEN

Technically you both work for the team

IMOGEN

You don't actually work in the same
department

SIENNA

Ooooh! 👣 👣 Excellent point, Imogen

You are not helping

SIENNA

You know my thoughts

IMOGEN

And mine

SIENNA

Clearly you want the same

SIENNA

So what are you waiting for?

DEEP BREATHS. I can do this. I can push Tag from my head.

Except…what if I don't want to?

A sexy man likes me and I'm ignoring him? *You're being stupid, Liv.* Just say yes.

What if I said yes?

What if my plan took a backseat for the time being and I said yes to the man that can make me orgasm without even being present?

New resolve in place, I answer my friends.

Fine. I'm doing it.

IMOGEN

You are?

SIENNA

You got this, love!

IMOGEN

Let us know how it goes

SIENNA

As if he'll say anything but yes

IMOGEN

You're gorgeous, darling

IMOGEN

And don't you forget it

xx

LOCKING MY PHONE, I set my bags down and head straight to Tag's office. I don't want to lose this newfound courage and chicken out if I sit and think about it all day.

I'm doing it. I'm saying yes.

Purposeful strides carry me across the building toward the coaches' offices. I can't remember the last time I felt so…in control of my own destiny.

With his office door in view, I give one swift knock before bursting in.

"Oh."

Tag. Standing in his office, a shirt in hand in all his half-naked glory. Those washboard abs I want to lick are on full display.

"Liv. What are you doing here?"

I don't think I got a good enough look that first night at Tag because these abs are even better than I remember.

"Liv?"

I shake myself out of the Tag-induced stupor. "Why are you changing in your office?"

He smirks back at me. "I didn't really intend on anyone busting in here when I was changing my shirt."

"Right. Well, I have a proposition for you."

"A proposition? Is that so?"

Thick biceps flex as they cross over his chest. His still bare chest.

"I'm sorry, can you please put your shirt on? It's very distracting to have all that there." I motion towards his chest.

"Continue."

Tag pulls the Lightning T-shirt in his hand over his head, running a hand through his messy hair.

"Here's my proposition." I clear my throat, trying not to let my nerves get the best of me. "I would like you to take me out on a date."

"You would?" Tag straightens, looking down at me. "Really?"

I nod. "Yes. I've decided that there is no reason why the two of us can't see one another."

"I'm not seeing the proposition here…" He trails off.

"I have a five-year plan. One that I don't want to get off track. And you have a job to do turning this team around. I see this as a way for mutual companionship and pleasure, and when it stops being that, we end things."

Tag smirks. "Mutual companionship and pleasure, hmm?"

"Yes. That's my proposition. Take it or leave it."

"Oh." Tag hooks a finger through the belt loop on my pants and tugs me close. "I'm taking it."

I collide with his chest, my hands landing on his pecs. "Good."

"I plan on taking you out tomorrow night."

"So soon?" I ask.

"Yes."

"Okay."

Tag is like me, jumping on this opportunity while he can. Because everything I said to him was true. I don't want this dalliance to come between us and our goals.

"Good plan," Tag agrees.

"Well then." I push off his chest. His eyes are alight with sparks. "I will see you tomorrow night."

"Plan on it."

From: Stanley Easton III <seaston@londonlightning.co.uk>
Sent: Tuesday, September 2, 2025 8:03 AM
To: Olivia Montrose <omontrose@londonlightning.co.uk>
Subject: Dinner

Liv,

Any thoughts as to where you would like to go to dinner tonight?

Thanks,
Stanley Easton III
Head Coach - London Lightning

From: Olivia Montrose <omontrose@londonlightning.co.uk>
Sent: Tuesday, September 2, 2025 8:11 AM
To: Stanley Easton III <seaston@londonlightning.co.uk>
Subject: RE: Dinner

Mr. Easton,

Surprise me.

Regards,

Olivia Montrose
Business Department
London Lightning

From: Stanley Easton III <seaston@londonlightning.co.uk>

Sent: Tuesday, September 2, 2025 8:15 AM
To: Olivia Montrose <omontrose@londonlightning.co.uk>
Subject: RE: Dinner

Surprise you? Can you at least tell me what you like?

Thanks,
Stanley Easton III
Head Coach - London Lightning

From: Olivia Montrose <omontrose@londonlight-
ning.co.uk>
Sent: Tuesday, September 2, 2025 8:32 AM
To: Stanley Easton III <seaston@londonlightning.co.uk>
Subject: RE: Dinner

Well, I liked the sandwiches you brought.

Regards,

Olivia Montrose
Business Department
London Lightning

From: Stanley Easton III <seaston@londonlight-
ning.co.uk>
Sent: Tuesday, September 2, 2025 8:45 AM
To: Olivia Montrose <omontrose@londonlightning.co.uk>
Subject: RE: Dinner

Sandwiches? I'm not going to take you to get sandwiches
for our date. It has to be something better than that.

Thanks,

Stanley Easton III
Head Coach - London Lightning

From: Olivia Montrose <omontrose@londonlight-
ning.co.uk>
Sent: Tuesday, September 2, 2025 8:52 AM
To: Stanley Easton III <seaston@londonlightning.co.uk>
Subject: RE: Dinner

Well, at least you know one thing not to do ;)

Regards,

Olivia Montrose
Business Department
London Lightning

From: Stanley Easton III <seaston@londonlight-
ning.co.uk>
Sent: Tuesday, September 2, 2025 9:05 AM
To: Olivia Montrose <omontrose@londonlightning.co.uk>
Subject: RE: Dinner

Don't you want to take pity on me? I don't know the good
places to go in London.

Thanks,
Stanley Easton III
Head Coach - London Lightning

From: Olivia Montrose <omontrose@londonlight-
ning.co.uk>
Sent: Tuesday, September 2, 2025 9:07 AM
To: Stanley Easton III <seaston@londonlightning.co.uk>

Subject: RE: Dinner

You know, there is this thing called the Internet. You can search there. Maybe exclude sandwiches.

Regards,

Olivia Montrose
Business Department
London Lightning

From: Stanley Easton III <seaston@londonlightning.co.uk>
Sent: Tuesday, September 2, 2025 9:10 AM
To: Olivia Montrose <omontrose@londonlightning.co.uk>
Subject: RE: Dinner

Damn, Liv. Way to call me out.

Thanks,
Stanley Easton III
Head Coach - London Lightning

From: Olivia Montrose <omontrose@londonlightning.co.uk>
Sent: Tuesday, September 2, 2025 9:13 AM
To: Stanley Easton III <seaston@londonlightning.co.uk>
Subject: RE: Dinner

Mr. Easton,

You have to work for it. If it helps, you know what I like to drink.

Regards,

Olivia Montrose
Business Department
London Lightning

From: Stanley Easton III <seaston@londonlight-
ning.co.uk>
Sent: Tuesday, September 2, 2025 9:17 AM
To: Olivia Montrose <omontrose@londonlightning.co.uk>
Subject: RE: Dinner

I don't plan on getting you drunk. I hope to have a repeat
of the night we met.

Thanks,
Stanley Easton III
Head Coach - London Lightning

From: Olivia Montrose <omontrose@londonlight-
ning.co.uk>
Sent: Tuesday, September 2, 2025 9:21 AM
To: Stanley Easton III <seaston@londonlightning.co.uk>
Subject: RE: Dinner

Tag! What have I said about keeping these emails
professional?

Regards,

Olivia Montrose
Business Department
London Lightning

From: Stanley Easton III <seaston@londonlight-
ning.co.uk>
Sent: Tuesday, September 2, 2025 9:27 AM
To: Olivia Montrose <omontrose@londonlightning.co.uk>
Subject: RE: Dinner

You brought it up.

Thanks,
Stanley Easton III
Head Coach - London Lightning

From: Olivia Montrose <omontrose@londonlight-
ning.co.uk>
Sent: Tuesday, September 2, 2025 9:30 AM
To: Stanley Easton III <seaston@londonlightning.co.uk>
Subject: RE: Dinner

Mr. Easton,

Do not make me reconsider our appointment.

Regards,

Olivia Montrose
Business Department
London Lightning

From: Stanley Easton III <seaston@londonlight-
ning.co.uk>
Sent: Tuesday, September 2, 2025 9:37 AM
To: Olivia Montrose <omontrose@londonlightning.co.uk>
Subject: RE: Dinner

Gotta go to practice. I'll see you for our "appointment."

Don't be late ;)

Chapter Nine

TAG

I can't remember the last time I've been so nervous for a first date. I don't even think I was this nervous for my first date with my wife.

Maybe that was the downfall of our marriage.

But it's the furthest thing from my mind as I fasten the last button on my dark blue shirt and tuck it into my black slacks. Complete with a fresh hair trim, I hope I look good. I even cleaned up my scruff so I'm ready for tonight.

I'm pulling out all the stops for Liv.

I have a feeling if I don't, she won't appreciate it. Even if she wouldn't let me pick her up. Settling to meet her at the restaurant was a compromise I didn't mind making for this night to happen.

I had to confer with Jack and Alfie about the best places in London. At least with them living here, they know these things.

Never would have pegged either of them for knowing a fancy French place, but I'll take it.

A cool wind moves around me, leaves crunching under

my feet. The sun sinks lower in the sky as it crawls toward the horizon.

Stuffing my hands in my pockets, I pick up my pace when the small restaurant comes into view. A green and white awning stretches over the sidewalk with a few café tables with patrons sitting close together.

But I'm stopped dead in my tracks when I see the woman standing outside waiting for me.

Checking my watch, I make sure I'm not late. Nope, ten minutes early.

Olivia looks stunning in skin-tight black jeans and a white camisole top with a bright pink blazer. I can't take my eyes off her.

"Damn, Liv. You look gorgeous." I lean in, pressing a kiss to her cheek. She smells even better. Like a bouquet of fresh flowers.

"Hi. You look nice," she tells me. Her appraising gaze wanders down my body. It makes me glad I put in the extra effort with how I look tonight.

Not that she minded me at the pub, but I want this date to go well.

"Thanks."

Opening the door to the restaurant, I place my hand at the small of her back and guide her inside.

Fresh baked bread. Herbs. Wine.

Everything smells delicious.

After giving the hostess my name, we're led through a maze of tables. The entire space is crammed full. People are rubbing elbows against the wall as we squeeze into one of the empty tables between two other couples.

"What do you think?" I ask Liv, taking the menu after helping her with her seat.

"Do you fancy French food?" she asks, eyes focused down on the menu.

"I thought you'd like it."

The man at the table next to us stands, bumping into ours and nearly knocking over the candle and water glasses. We're packed in tighter than sardines.

After discussing the date with Jack and Alfie, they agreed that something nicer would be best. And since my knowledge of good places to take a date in London is approximately zero, I trusted their judgment.

"Umm, Tag?"

"Yeah?"

"Do you know what half of these words even mean?" she asks, finger skimming down the menu, eyes following it.

I don't recognize the first three things on the menu, let alone how to pronounce them.

"I think frites is fries."

Liv snickers, burying her face in the menu. "Can I ask why you brought me here if you don't like French food?"

"Shit." I set the menu down and study her. There's a playful smile on her face. Her hair is fixed into a fancy contraption at the nape of her neck. "The guys were helping me, and I thought you'd like this kind of place."

"I like that you put in the effort," she starts.

"I feel like there is a but coming."

Liv shuts her menu and leans across the table. With the small candle in the middle of the table, it makes her glow. "But I don't need anything fancy. I like simple."

"Really?"

Liv stands and drops her napkin onto the table. "Come on. I'll show you what I really like doing on a first date." Following suit, I pull a couple of bills out of my wallet and drop them on the table.

It's still funny to me seeing the different money.

"Does this mean I fail at the first date?" I ask her, holding the door open for her and walking out of the restaurant. The hostess who just sat us has a confused look on her face. Like she is wondering why anyone would ever want to leave the restaurant here without eating.

"Well, there's still time to recover," she says.

"Lead the way."

A coolness has settled over the city now that the sun has almost set. I follow Liv as she walks toward the river and hangs a right, putting the Tower Bridge behind us.

"You know, this is one of the things I like most about the city so far," I tell Liv.

"The river?"

I nod, draping an arm over Liv's shoulders. "It reminds me of Nashville."

"Tell me about Nashville."

Throngs of people are heading in the opposite direction of us. I couldn't care less about what sights I'm missing.

I'm happy to be with Liv tonight.

"I loved that there is always something to do. Kind of like here. Live music, sports. Nashville has it all. With a lot more humidity."

"Hey." Liv elbows me in the side. "It's humid here. Just wait until it rains."

"On the hot summer days, all the guys and I would head out of the city with inner tubes and just float down a river with some beers. I loved it."

"You floated down the river?" She looks at me like I have three heads. "I don't know if I've ever heard of that, let alone done it. I can't say that is one of London's great pastimes. Nor would anyone want to do it in the Thames."

"Maybe that could be a second date for us."

"Oh?" Liv looks up at me, wrapping her arm around my waist. "You're assuming this date is going well enough to lead to another?"

God, I can't get over those blue eyes of hers. I don't know how they suck me in, but every time I see them turned on me, it does funny things to my insides.

"I'm hedging my bets. No French restaurants."

"Good. Because here we are."

Liv stops in front of one of the most unassuming places on the side of the river. A shack, really. If I can call it that.

The clapboard structure is painted blue and white with a window thrown open in the front. An older man is standing there, taking orders.

"This is where you want to eat?"

Liv nods and steps into line. "Don't knock it until you try it."

"I'll trust your judgment, my little Londoner."

She beams up at me before moving to the window. "Hi, Mr. Ramsey."

"Oy, Liv. My favorite customer. How are you tonight?"

His accent is thick, much thicker than I'm used to.

"I'm good. I'm getting dinner with my friend tonight. He's new in town."

Friend? I don't know if that's going to fly, but hey, she's already talked about a second date, so maybe this is going well. Well, at least until I get her to agree to said date.

"I'm showing him the best London has to offer."

"Well, you brought him to the right place." He gives her a toothy grin as she orders fish and chips for each of us. Pulling out a crisp, twenty-pound note, I pass it over and tell him to keep the change.

"Thanks, mate. Liv taking good care of ya?"

"She is. After I took her to quite possibly the worst restaurant ever."

"It wasn't the worst," she confesses. "It's not my taste."

"This one is not easy to please," Mr. Ramsey says, handing over two paper plates with large slabs of fish and crisp chips. "But once you know the way to her heart, it's easy."

"Good to know."

Taking the plates, I tip my head in his direction and follow Liv to a picnic bench next to the building. Two single lampposts light up the small patio area.

"This is your favorite place in London?" I ask, setting her plate in front of her.

"It is." She grabs the vinegar on the table and pours it on. "Here. You have to eat it the correct way."

"With vinegar?"

She nods. "Trust me."

"Oh, I do."

Grabbing a piece of fish, I bring it to my mouth and take a bite. It's hot, fried, and absolutely delicious. "Damn. This really might be the best thing I've had since I got here."

"Told you." Liv uses a fork and knife to cut into a piece and pops it in her mouth.

"How'd you discover this place?"

"I stumbled upon it one day while exploring the area after I moved here. Mr. Ramsey was easy to talk with and I've been coming back ever since."

"Well, maybe I will sweet-talk Mr. Ramsey into letting me bring this to the office for our next lunch. That is, if you'll let me."

Liv bites another tiny piece off her fork and chews, pondering my statement. "As long as there is no French food, you can bring me lunch."

"Done."

I don't try to hide my smile as I eat faster than most would be considered polite. But after ditching our original spot, I've starving.

"Good, right?" Liv asks.

"You really know where to take a guy."

"Speaking of which…"

"Yes?" I reach across the table and grab a napkin from her pile, wiping the excess vinegar off my fingers.

"If you would like a tour of the city, I would be happy to take you."

"Really?" I quirk a brow at her. "Decided you would be the best tour guide for me after all?"

"I still think you would be better served with an *actual* tour guide, but it would be fun."

"I can guarantee I will have a better time with you than anyone else."

Liv sets her knife and fork down on the side of her plate. She is so proper, it makes me like her that much more. She fishes around in her purse and pulls out two sticks of gum, handing one over to me.

"Would you like to continue this good time then?"

That piques my interest. I take the gum and pop it into my mouth, watching as she does the same.

"What did you have in mind? Dessert? Drinks? Going back to your apartment?"

"Tag." There's the long-suffering sigh I know and love from her. I shouldn't enjoy eliciting this response from her, but I do. "You know it's a flat."

"Sorry. This flat of yours. Will it be nice and neat?"

"And if it is?"

"I can't wait to mess it up."

Chapter Ten

OLIVIA

The walk back to my flat feels longer than it should. With Tag's hand in mine, I'm anxious. Not because I'm nervous about what is about to happen.

No.

I'm excited.

I told myself before I left that I wouldn't feel pressured into going home with him if he asked. We've already had sex. I know it's good. No, great.

Turns out, it was me who couldn't contain herself when it came to Tag.

"This is me," I tell Tag once my building comes into view. He squeezes my hand in response as I key open the front door and step inside. A short, brightly lit hall leads back to my unit.

"Looks nice." Tag gives my flat an appraising eye as I follow him inside.

Refurbished hardwood floors have a natural finish to them. A small bookcase is built into the back wall that overlooks a small garden. The kitchen isn't much, with a small washer thrown in, but at least my bedroom is cosy.

"It's not much, but I like having access to my own green space. Something a lot of Londoners don't necessarily have." I slip out of my blazer and drape it over the back of the sofa, not before grabbing the gum wrapper and spitting the piece out.

"I don't want to talk about London real estate." Tag grabs me around the waist and pulls me into him.

"No?"

He shakes his head. "I'm more interested in messing up this flat of yours."

"Then let me lead the way." Stepping out of his arms, I grab his hand and lead him towards my bedroom.

It's not overly large, but the bed is brimming with pillows and a soft duvet. It's welcoming with pinks and yellows against the grey wall. It's my sanctuary.

In the soft light of the room, Tag looks hungry. Like he wants to devour me. The entire walk home all I could think about was getting his mouth on mine.

"Sit on the bed."

"What?" he asks, looking a tiny bit stunned.

"I believe you heard me."

"Look at you." His warm hand doesn't leave my side as he takes me with him, plopping down on the side of the bed. "Taking control."

"I know what I want."

"And what's that?"

Stepping between his spread legs, I cup his cheeks and press my lips against his. His response is immediate, opening for me as I slide my tongue against his. He tastes like the gum he's been chewing. I'm not sure when he ditched his, but I'm greedy. Sucking on his tongue and drinking him in.

Liquid heat flashes through my veins as his fingers slip

under the hem of my satin top. How can a kiss be even better than I remembered it?

Lust fogs my head as I get swept up in his kiss.

Strong hands pull me down onto his lap. A gasp escapes my lips at the feel of his hard cock between my legs.

"Tag."

"Do you know how good you taste?" He purrs against my neck. "I can't fucking wait to taste your sweet, sweet pussy again."

"I want to taste you." I throw my head back as Tag's lips trail a warm, wet path down my chest.

"I think I can make that happen."

Tag's cock twitches between my legs as he wraps an arm around my waist and tosses me down onto the bed.

"Oh!"

Towering above me, Tag's presence fills my vision. His hand rubs over his hard length before deft fingers undo the buttons of his shirt. Sitting up, I pull the camisole over my head.

Before I can unfasten my bra, Tag stops me with a hand to my chest. "That's my job, baby."

His hands drift upward, finding the hook and flicking it. I let my bra slide down my arms as Tag's eyes take in my naked chest. My nipples are tight under his slow perusal.

"It seems unfair that you're not getting naked too," I tell him.

"I'll get there." One lone finger drags a trail up the center of my chest, tracing the bare skin there. "I've been dreaming about your body since that night."

"Yeah?" I squirm under his intense stare, needing more relief than he is giving me.

"I love how responsive you are to me." His fingers

pluck my nipple. "How I know exactly what to do to make you wet."

"I'm not wet."

It's a blatant lie, but if it moves things along, I'll be happy. I'm aching and want Tag.

Covering my body with his, Tag whispers in my ear, "Now why does that sound like a lie?"

"Is it?" I fire back.

His hand drifts low, cupping my pussy through my jeans. "I think it's time I found out if you are lying."

Tag makes quick work of my heels, jeans, and underwear. But not before he fingers the soft material.

"I knew it," he says. "Are you ready for me, Liv?"

"God, yes."

Strong hands move over my legs. I'm becoming obsessed with the feel of Tag's hands on my bare skin. The way they caress me. As if he's studying for an exam to recall every inch of my body.

"Tag." Grabbing his wrist, I stop the trailing of his hand as it moves farther up my body, now hovering on my soft stomach.

"What, baby?" Lips nibble at the soft skin of my neck.

"You're going the wrong way."

"Is that so? You want my hands here?"

Calloused fingers massage the muscles in my calves.

"No."

"Here?" A single finger drags over the back of my knee. "Or here?"

They slide down the backs of my thighs, stopping just before the tips of his fingers hit my arse.

"Keep going."

I'm wet, pussy throbbing as the man above me winds me up tighter and tighter. I'm a live wire ready to snap.

"Tag," I groan. "Please."

"Is this what you want?" He sinks one long, thick finger inside of me and I nearly combust with the pleasure of it.

"Yes!" I gasp.

His moves are slow and measured as I chase down the heat that curls inside of me. It won't take much for him to push me over the edge.

I'm a writhing mess underneath him as his mouth captures mine and our tongues tangle. My nails dig into his back, urging him on.

"Are you going to come for me like I know you can?"

"Make me."

Tag nips at the tender skin of my neck. It feels so good with his finger thrusting inside me that I can't hold it together a minute longer.

I come unglued. If it weren't for Tag's weight holding me down, I feel like I could fly off the bed. Stars burst behind my eyes as words of praise rain down on me from the man working me through my orgasm.

"So fucking good, Liv. So wet. So perfect. Fuck. I can't wait to suck your release off my fingers."

"I want more," I purr.

"So greedy."

Tag seals his mouth over mine. He tries to pull back, but I don't let him. I need his touch as my body comes down from the most perfect orgasm I've ever had.

"Only because you make me feel so incredible."

"Well." Tag tucks a lock of hair behind my ear. "Get ready, because I will be making you feel more of that."

This time, I do push him back. "Not until I get my taste."

Shoving him onto his back, I shed him of his remaining clothing and watch as his dick springs free. Licking my lips, I can't take my eyes off his hard length.

The way the vein on the underside throbs. The precum

leaking from the tip. It's a heady sensation knowing that I'm the one that makes this sexy specimen of a man feel this way.

"What are you waiting for? Do it," he urges me on.

I quirk a brow at him. "Now who's being greedy?"

"I can't help it if I'm ready to fuck you again. I've only been waiting since you left my bed the first night."

I smile up at him as I take his cock in hand. "I won't be leaving tomorrow morning, that I can promise."

"Fuck. That feels good."

"It'll feel even better in a minute."

Sucking the tip into my mouth, I swirl my tongue around the head, loving the sounds that escape Tag.

I take him as far back as I can, stretching my lips around his girth. The salty taste of him on my tongue urges me on. Bringing a man like Tag Easton to his knees has me swallowing him back as far as I can.

"Fuuuuck." Tag thrusts up into my mouth, causing me to gag around him. "Fuck, sorry, baby."

I pull off him. "Don't be."

Taking a deep breath, I dive back on him. Using my hand and mouth, I work him over in hard squeezes and long, slow sucks. I lap up everything he is giving me. Until his fingers card through my hair and pull me off him with a pop.

"Now. I want to be inside that sweet pussy of yours *now*."

"Condom?" I ask.

"Wallet."

Finding his jeans on the floor, I fish it out of his pocket and take out the foiled packet. I make quick work of opening it and sliding it down him.

Before he can move, I'm straddling his hips. I line

myself up and slide down his cock, allowing time to adjust to his thick size.

I'm wet from my earlier release, making it easier as I take him fully inside me.

"Yes." I dig my nails into his pecs as I wiggle my hips.

Rocking over him, my moves are slow and measured. Every inch of him feels like he was made just for me.

"Fuck, Liv. You look so damn beautiful like this." Tag pulls me down, wiping the corner of my mouth before leaning in for a searing kiss. "Bouncing on my cock."

"I can't get enough. I'm so close."

"Then come."

Tag grabs my hips and pumps up—hard—into me. "Oh!"

My orgasm is no less powerful than before as it sweeps through me. It's as if my own release drags his out of him. I collapse on top of him as he fills the condom.

"Baby, that was so damn good."

His bare skin is sticky under mine. Our breathing syncs as we both come down from our highs.

I'm becoming addicted to being in his arms like this. I want more.

Even if it's not in the plan.

Chapter Eleven

TAG

Stretching my muscles, I flip over in bed. I can't help the smile that spreads across my face.

Last night with Liv might have been the best night I've had since coming to London. Hell, the best night I've had in a long time.

The sounds coming from the other room, and the cold bed beside me, tell me Liv has been up for a while.

Glancing at the clock, it's still early. Thank God for a late practice today, because I'm hoping I can convince Liv to go another round before I have to leave.

The woman in question walks in from the kitchen, two mugs in her hand. In only the shirt I was wearing last night and mussed-up hair, she looks sexy as hell.

Especially as she chews on her bottom lip.

"Morning."

Sitting up, the duvet falls from my chest as Liv sits down next to me. Strong coffee scents the air.

"Morning." I sip the hot brew, letting it wake me up, even though I feel fucking amazing after last night.

"Sleep well?"

Grabbing both cups, I set them on the nightstand and pull her into me. "Great. Especially since I got to share the bed with you."

Sealing our mouths together, I let my tongue tangle with hers. Damn, if I could wake up like this every morning, I'd be a happy man.

"You know we have to get to work," Liv tells me, even though she makes no move to get up.

"It's a good thing practice doesn't start until later today."

She quirks a brow at me. "Did you plan that on purpose?"

I shake my head. "Not at all. When do you have to be in?"

Liv glances at the clock on her dresser. "In an hour."

Sliding a hand up and under her shirt, I nip at her neck. "Does that mean you have time for a quickie?"

Her skin is so warm and so damn soft that I'm having trouble hearing her words. All I want to do is bury myself inside of her again.

"Are you listening?" She grabs my cheeks and pulls my focus to her.

"It's hard to when you're underneath me."

"I asked how this is going to work."

"What do you mean?" That has me confused.

"I mean, you and I work together."

"In the same building," I correct. "It's not like you're my employee. There's no direct line of reporting. It's fine."

She sighs. "More like I don't want things to be weird between us when others are around."

I straddle her hips, settling my weight fully on top of her. "I do not plan on making things weird at work. Do you?"

She shakes her head. "No."

Even though I have a feeling it will be weird for her when she sees me at work today. Not that the likelihood of the two of us bumping into each other is high, but I have a feeling she'll still be awkward.

Add this to the list of things I like about her so much.

"Good." My fingers work open the buttons on her shirt. "Then I am going to fuck you senseless, so I know you'll have something else to focus on at work."

Chapter Twelve

TAG

"You know, when you said team bonding, this isn't quite what I had in mind."

"What did you have in mind?" I ask.

After another shitty practice, I couldn't let the team keep spiraling. They're not gelling, and it's only going to get worse if I don't step in and do something.

"I don't know. I figured it'd be like the things they used to make us do at summer camp. Like trust falls or what have you."

I laugh. "I don't think that would work out too well with these guys. We need to build up to that."

"Smashing things is better?" Jack quirks a brow at me. "Do you think this is going to work?"

I shrug a shoulder. "Fuck all if I know. But it'll be a start."

When I first tried to come up with a place to bring the team together, I wasn't really thinking of a smash room. But the more I looked at it, the more I figured why not try? Bringing a bunch of men together to blow shit up?

Who wouldn't love that?

I can feel their skepticism as I drop my wallet, keys, and phone into the small lock box. The younger woman who works here is busy handing out face shields—attached to a hard hat—to all the guys.

"You know, I think this could work," Alfie says.

"Glad you don't think I'm crazy."

I grab the proffered shield as I enter the room. This one is more tame than some of the others I've seen. Considering we have our first game next week, I wanted this to be a safe event for the guys.

Graffiti paints the wood walls. Old TVs, pallets, glassware, and furniture cover the space. Everything is in here for us to destroy.

A ripple of excitement works its way through the guys as a brief safety demonstration is given.

Mainly, check to make sure you have room to swing your chosen tool before doing so. I can't imagine getting clocked in the head with a sledgehammer.

Alfie elbows me in the side. "You think you'd want to bring your new girl here?"

I roll my eyes at him. "I never should have told you I was taking her out."

"I still can't believe you didn't tell me," Jack whispers.

"It's because you didn't want to join us that night," Alfie oh-so-helpfully supplies.

"Wasn't my fault my train was delayed."

"Either way, I regret it." I laugh.

Jack flips me off as we move to a corner to let the guys get a head start. With only so many sledgehammers, they're going to be taking turns.

"No, you don't," Jack says. "You like telling us things."

"Not in the company of the team. They don't need to know about my love life."

"That means things are going well?" Alfie asks.

"We've only had one date."

Even though it went really well, I still don't want to divulge too much about it to these guys.

Cracks and bangs echo around the room as the players get started. Whoops and shouts ring out.

"Damn. It looks like they're really liking this," Jack tells me.

"See? I wasn't lying."

I had no idea how this would go, but it's clear they are liking it. Hell, seeing the smiles on their faces has me thinking this might be a good place to bring Liv.

If only to see her let her hair down.

"Think we need to be concerned with Simmons?" Jack asks, nodding toward our goalie, who is pounding away on what appears to be an old trash can.

Glancing across the room, I find the man in question.

At the rate he's going, he is going to demolish the sledgehammer he's using. Considering we were the most scored upon team last year, his anger is justified.

"I'll check on him after."

I watch as the guys keep smashing the room to smithereens. Bits of debris fly around—thank God for the helmets, because I don't want anyone getting injured.

"Hey, Coach. You want a turn?"

McCord, the newest player we got in a trade with Belfast, holds out a baseball bat to me.

"Hell, yeah."

Safety shield firmly in place, I grab the bat and find something that isn't ripped to shreds. A lone TV sits in the corner untouched.

Winding up the bat, I take a swing.

Glass and plastic explode from the tip of the bat as it shatters the small screen. *Fuck, yeah.*

I don't let a single piece of it out of my sight as I swing

and swing. The cracks and explosions from around the room are music to my ears.

"Do you have your own issues to work out?" Alfie questions as I wipe the sweat from my brow.

"Nah. It just feels good." I hold out the bat to him. "You do it."

Alfie grabs the bat and Jack takes a sledgehammer from another guy. Between the two of them, they work out their aggression on an old trash can.

By the end of our hour, not a single thing is left intact. Guys are stepping over scraps of what was once a TV. Glass. Wood.

"How'd that feel?" I ask the guys as we head back into the dining area off the smash room.

"Fucking awesome. I wish we could do this every week."

Pizza and buckets of beer sit on the tables stretching across the room. The walls in here are like the ones in the smash room—covered in graffiti in bright oranges and yellows.

TVs hang in the corners with videos of people tearing various rooms up. The guys immediately go for the drinks and stand around chatting, reliving what they just did based on their gestures.

"Simmons." I walk over to our goalie and pull him away from the other defensemen on the team. "How are you feeling?"

He beams bright and happy at me. "Honestly? Fucking amazing."

"Good. I'm glad."

"I've never done anything like this with another team before," he tells me.

"I've never done anything like this in my life." I laugh.

Simmons eyes me warily, like he's weighing if he can trust me with what he's about to say.

"I'm really trying, Coach. I think my glove skills are getting better. Coach Alfie is helping me a lot."

"Good, I'm glad he is. You're improving, and sometimes it might not feel like you're doing it as fast as you want to, but we're all seeing it."

He nods. "I'm going to keep working hard to show you I can do it."

"I know you'll keep it up." I clap him on the shoulder. "Now, go grab something to eat before these guys eat it all."

He smiles at me before joining the rest of the team.

I never envied the goalie on our team. Much like Simmons, we were one of the most scored upon teams in the league.

We sucked. Plain and simple. I never wanted to be the one to carry the loss for letting the goals in. It's something every goalie carries with them, Simmons included. It's like every goal scored on them is a dent in their pads they wear.

"Guess you were right," Alfie tells me, pulling me from my thoughts.

"I knew he'd be okay. Credited you for his turnaround."

"Really?"

Alfie looks shocked at this news, his face turning the color of a tomato.

"Said it's because he's been training with you. Just what we like to hear about our coaches."

"It's not me." Alfie shies away from the praise. "He's got skill. Just needs someone to help him harness it out on the ice."

"Doesn't hurt that he has a good coach."

His blush darkens as he walks away from me to the safety of Jack and starts chatting with him.

Looking around the room, it seems I achieved my goal. We'll see if it translates to the ice before our first game next week. With only one more practice to go, I hope it does.

Now that Liv and I are dating, I'm liking my new home here in London. Not that I wasn't going to do a good job before, but I want to stick around.

Because I like Liv and want to see where this thing goes.

Chapter Thirteen

OLIVIA

Checking the time again, I try not to worry that Tag is running late. Having wanted to show him another one of my favourite places in the city, I planned it when we could be alone. But with a late practise in the afternoon for him, we're cutting it close.

My phone vibrates in my pocket. Half expecting it to be Tag cancelling, I'm shocked at the name that pops up.

Mum.

Not wasting a second, I slide my thumb across the screen to answer the call. "Hello, Mum."

"Olivia. How are you?" Her prim and proper voice is quiet over the phone.

"I'm well. And you?"

"Also well." She clears her throat. "I was returning your call."

"My call?"

"Yes, Olivia." She gives an annoyed sigh. "You rang a few weeks ago."

I try not to let my own annoyance with my mother take

hold. I called weeks ago and never got a call back. Now somehow it's my fault that she is just calling me back?

"Right. How are things at home?"

"Fine. Your father is good. I am good. All is good."

"Right. Things are good here as well."

It's the most stilted call I've ever had with her.

"And your job? You are still working for the hockey team?" Her voice is dripping with disdain. When I told them where I would be working, they turned their noses up.

Working for a hockey team is not a suitable position for their daughter.

"I am. I'm enjoying it. Learning a lot."

"Good. And any suitable men you're dating?"

Suitable? I don't know if I would describe Tag as suitable. At least in their eye. A divorced man from America working for the team? They would hate him.

"Not at the moment."

The lie feels sour on my tongue.

"Well, you don't want to wait too long."

"Yes, Mum," I agree, only because it's the easiest thing to do.

"Well, then. We've been on the phone too long. Speak soon."

She hangs up before I can get another word in.

One minute and ten seconds. That's how long my phone tells me the call lasted. Too long for my own mum.

I try not to let my emotions take over as I stuff my phone in my coat pocket. I should consider it a positive that she even took the time to call me back, even if it was weeks later.

"Hey, baby."

Tag is striding towards me, eating up the distance on the sidewalk. The sight of him soothes my frayed nerves.

"Hi."

He greets me with a kiss. "You know, when you said you wanted to show me some hidden sights of London, I didn't think it would be this hidden."

"You don't like parks?"

Tag shakes his head, draping his arm around my shoulder. "That's not it at all. I'm just surprised, is all."

It's a brisk Thursday night. The park is all but empty as we walk through the entry gate. Burrowing closer to Tag, I steer him farther inside the garden. With fall here, not much is in bloom, but it's still one of my favourite spots in London.

Since I really need to clear my head after that call with Mum, I am glad that I brought Tag here tonight.

"Because everything is dead and it'd be prettier in the spring?" I gaze up at Tag. His eyes are already focused on me. They always are. No matter where we are, whenever we're together, I can feel his gaze on me.

"Well, yeah."

"It's my favourite, so I wanted to bring you here."

Tag presses his lips to the top of my head. Warmth spreads through me at the slight touch. "I like that you want to bring me to your favorite places."

"It's peaceful here. Like I can put the chaos of the city in the back of my mind and just relax."

And the chaos of my own family, but I don't tell him that. Too heavy for this thing between the two of us.

Finding a bench, I sit down and pull Tag with me.

"I can understand that. This city is a lot different from Nashville, but I'm adjusting better than I thought."

Resting my chin on his shoulder, I stare up at Tag. "Really? I couldn't imagine moving to another country."

Tag grabs my hand, holding it in his large, warm palm. His fingers trace patterns into my soft skin.

It's soothing. Mesmerising.

"You've helped with it."

"Yeah?" I rest my head on his shoulder.

"Yeah." His warm breath ghosts across my forehead. "You've made it easy. Welcoming me. Showing me around. Just being you."

"I'm glad I could help then."

Tag's thumb presses into the racing pulse of my wrist. "I thought I was running away after my divorce, but turns out, I don't think I was."

Shifting, I turn to look at Tag. "You don't really talk about your divorce."

He shrugs. "It's not something that I really like to talk about."

"You don't have to."

"It's okay. We met when we were in college. I suppose at some point we were in love, but then it just became more about staying with someone when I got drafted. I didn't want to deal with the whole dating scene while playing. And then when I stopped playing, she didn't like that I gave up the life."

"Does that make you sad?"

He shakes his head, turning to face me. "At first, it did. But then after therapy, I realized I was better off on my own than being in a loveless marriage."

"I guess with age comes wisdom."

Tag bursts out laughing and I love the sound of it. "Don't get me wrong, I was opposed to the idea at first, but I like it."

"Therapy? I don't know if I could ever spill my guts out to anyone like that."

Tag smiles at me. "It's oddly refreshing."

"Ripping open your emotions for a stranger? No, thanks."

"Okay." Tag shifts, tucking a wind-blown strand of hair behind my ear. "Why don't you try talking to me? Tell me something no one else knows about you."

"That is quite the change in conversation."

"You don't want to talk to a stranger, so talk to me."

It's hard to get a read on his brown eyes. The sun continues its slow descent towards the horizon. Before long, we'll be kicked out of here.

Not the worst thing right now.

Something no one else knows about me?

There's a lot I could tell him. My childhood. Growing up with my parents. That seems too heavy for what we're doing.

How a one-minute phone call was too long for my mother.

This is supposed to be fun. Nothing serious.

So what can I tell this man that won't open up a floodgate of emotions inside of me?

"I hate heights."

"Really? In the whole wide world of things you could have told me, that's what you chose to go with?"

"Hey." I poke him in the side. "You said tell you something no one else knows. No one knows that."

"Okay. You don't like heights. Something new to put in my encyclopedia of everything Olivia Montrose."

"I like keeping my feet firmly on solid ground."

"I guess that explains why you said no to skydiving."

A shudder racks my body. "There is no way in hell I would ever do that. I can't believe you would!"

Tag leans back against the bench, resting his arm along the back. "Why not?"

"Why not?" I scoff. "What if the parachute doesn't work? Or something happens to the plane? I prefer not splatting into the ground like a pancake."

Tag smiles at me. "I know what *not* to plan for our next date then."

"'Scuse me. Park is closing." An old man in a uniform walks through, pointing at his watch. "Time to go."

"Thank you," I tell him, standing to grab Tag's hand.

We're the only ones in here as we walk towards the exit. It's like being in our own little cocoon in the busy city.

Maybe it's why I felt safe confessing something—even if it wasn't a deep, dark secret—to Tag. Or maybe that's just Tag.

"Hey." Tag stops me outside the locked gate. "Thanks for telling me something no one else knows about you."

"Thank you for making it easy."

I wish I could gather up the courage to confess more to this man. But for now, this will do.

From: Olivia Montrose <omontrose@londonlight-
ning.co.uk>
Sent: Friday, September 26, 2025 10:03 AM
To: Stanley Easton III <seaston@londonlightning.co.uk>
Subject: Good Luck

Mr. Easton,

I wanted to wish you luck at the game tomorrow night
against Edinburgh. They're a good team, but hopefully you
can beat them. Looking forward to your return.

Regards,

Olivia Montrose
Business Department
London Lightning

From: Stanley Easton III <seaston@londonlight-
ning.co.uk>
Sent: Friday, September 26, 2025 10:07 AM
To: Olivia Montrose <omontrose@londonlightning.co.uk>
Subject: RE: Good Luck

Liv,

Looking forward to my return, is that right?

PS — Like the signature? Very professional, right? You
haven't said anything about it yet.

Thanks,

Stanley Easton III
Head Coach - London Lightning

From: Olivia Montrose <omontrose@londonlight-ning.co.uk>
Sent: Friday, September 26, 2025 10:21 AM
To: Stanley Easton III <seaston@londonlightning.co.uk>
Subject: RE: Good Luck

Mr. Easton,

If you have to point out how professional it is, is that actually the case?

Regards,

Olivia Montrose
Business Department
London Lightning

From: Stanley Easton III <seaston@londonlight-ning.co.uk>
Sent: Friday, September 26, 2025 10:38 AM
To: Olivia Montrose <omontrose@londonlightning.co.uk>
Subject: RE: Good Luck

I am very professional. I don't know what you're talking about.

Are you going to be watching the game?

Thanks,
Stanley Easton III

Head Coach - London Lightning

From: Olivia Montrose <omontrose@londonlightning.co.uk>
Sent: Friday, September 26, 2025 10:52 AM
To: Stanley Easton III <seaston@londonlightning.co.uk>
Subject: RE: Good Luck

The games are not on TV here, so I can't watch it. If you're not aware, football is the most popular sport here. But I'll be wishing you the best of luck from afar.

Regards,

Olivia Montrose
Business Department
London Lightning

From: Stanley Easton III <seaston@londonlightning.co.uk>
Sent: Friday, September 26, 2025 12:52 PM
To: Olivia Montrose <omontrose@londonlightning.co.uk>
Subject: RE: Good Luck

Ouch. Football is the most popular sport? Are you setting me up to lose?

Thanks,
Stanley Easton III
Head Coach - London Lightning

From: Olivia Montrose <omontrose@londonlightning.co.uk>

Sent: Friday, September 26, 2025 1:03 PM
To: Stanley Easton III <seaston@londonlightning.co.uk>
Subject: RE: Good Luck

I'm only saying it for you to manage expectations, Tag. Not a lot of people come to the games here. Not setting you up to lose. Just…keep that in mind.

Regards,

Olivia Montrose
Business Department
London Lightning

From: Stanley Easton III <seaston@londonlightning.co.uk>
Sent: Friday, September 26, 2025 1:15 PM
To: Olivia Montrose <omontrose@londonlightning.co.uk>
Subject: RE: Good Luck

Like how many people? You know, just to manage my expectations.

Thanks,
Stanley Easton III
Head Coach - London Lightning

From: Olivia Montrose <omontrose@londonlightning.co.uk>
Sent: Friday, September 26, 2025 1:23 PM
To: Stanley Easton III <seaston@londonlightning.co.uk>
Subject: RE: Good Luck

Not nearly as many as you're used to. Now, go prepare for the game. I want to see you win.

Good luck,

Olivia Montrose
Business Department
London Lightning

From: Stanley Easton III <seaston@londonlight-ning.co.uk>
Sent: Friday, September 26, 2025 1:25 PM
To: Olivia Montrose <omontrose@londonlightning.co.uk>
Subject: RE: Good Luck

Hey, no jinxing us! No talk of winning just yet.

Thanks,
Stanley Easton III
Head Coach - London Lightning

From: Olivia Montrose <omontrose@londonlight-ning.co.uk>
Sent: Friday, September 26, 2025 1:33 PM
To: Stanley Easton III <seaston@londonlightning.co.uk>
Subject: RE: Good Luck

Fine. Then back to my original sentiments…good luck.

Olivia Montrose
Business Department
London Lightning

From: Stanley Easton III <seaston@londonlight-
ning.co.uk>
Sent: Friday, September 26, 2025 1:45 PM
To: Olivia Montrose <omontrose@londonlightning.co.uk>
Subject: RE: Good Luck

Thanks, Liv. See you when we get home ;)

Thanks,
Stanley Easton III
Head Coach - London Lightning

Chapter Fourteen

TAG

The first game of the season is finally here. It's always my favorite time of the year.

There's no wins and losses yet. Everyone is starting out as equals. We've got a clean slate and have the entire season laid out ahead of us.

The guys are all joshing around together in the visitors' locker room. Hard folding chairs sit between metal lockers. Harsh overhead lights glare down on us.

The sense of excitement and nerves is palpable.

"All right, men. Are you ready?" I call out.

"Hell, yeah!"

"Let's fucking go!"

"We've got this!"

Cheers echo all around me in the locker room. It's the kind of energy I love seeing before a game. Practice has gotten better since our bonding event. We still have a long way to go, but I like what I'm seeing.

"Edinburgh has a good team. I'm not going to deny that. I want you to use everything we've learned in practice and work together as a team."

I look around the room and take in my team. A frenetic energy is coursing through them. "We're ready. Go out there and play your game. Don't try to do anything extra or fancy. Just do what you do."

Jack and Alfie are nodding along next to me as I finish my pregame speech.

Simmons pulls everyone together in the center of the room. "You heard Coach. Play our game and do what we do. Lightning on three. One, two…"

"Lightning!"

Guys grab their sticks and helmets and head down the tunnel toward the ice. Seeing as how this is my very first EIHL game, I don't know what I'm in for.

But what I see when I get out there shocks me.

The arena is smaller. I knew that. But based on Liv's emails, I assumed it would be a crowd of a dozen or so people.

This? This is not that.

The entire place is packed to the brim with people as boos ring out to signal our arrival. Signs are held aloft for the various members of the home team. The Eagles logo is splashed across every surface in black, yellow, and white.

"Damn."

"Not quite the NHL?" Jack asks as we take our positions on the bench.

"More people than I thought."

"Really?" he asks, looking thoroughly confused.

I nod. "Liv made it sound like there wouldn't be anyone here."

"Edinburgh brings in a pretty large crowd. But there's a good number of Lightning fans here for an away game. They believe we are going to turn this team around."

"Damn right we are."

Because I want nothing more than to prove to Liv that

we can do it. That we can be a team like Edinburgh and bring the people in.

The music changes and the crowd gets louder. In the small space, it causes my ears to ring. Edinburgh takes the ice to raucous applause and cheers.

Before the game starts, the UK's national anthem plays throughout the arena. That's something that is definitely going to take some getting used to.

Before I know it, the puck drops and the game starts.

Within seconds, it's easy to see why Edinburgh is one of the top teams in the league year in and year out.

Even with the progress we've been making in practice, we can't keep up. In what seems like no time at all, the Eagles get an easy pass and are flying toward our end of the ice. Snapping my eyes to Simmons, he tightens up. I can see him reading the winger but before we can make a move, the puck is flying over his shoulder, lighting the lamp.

Fuck.

I glance at the scoreboard—they scored in under two minutes. It could be a very long night if it continues like this.

When play resumes, our guys are on top of them, but it's hard to steal the puck and get into their zone.

McCord intercepts an easy pass and takes off on a breakaway, but their goalie is primed and ready. He snatches the puck out of thin air before it can cross the goal line.

"That's okay, boys. That was a great play. Let's draw up more plays like that—good defense and we'll capitalize on it."

I walk up and down the bench encouraging everyone as the lines change. We have a few more missed passes, and another easy goal slips in, but the guys are skating better together.

Before the first period ends, their hard work finally pays off. With a slick defensive move, Gavin shoots the puck up to McCord. With Jessup, another winger, skating with him, the two of them are able to work together to score.

"Hell, yeah!" I pump my arm as the guys all stand to bang their sticks on the boards. "Great job!"

When the horn sounds, I'm happy as the guys file into the locker room.

"Alright, men. That was a great first period. You made the necessary changes on the ice to clean up play. They might have gotten off to a fast start, but Simmons?" I look around for our goalie. "Simmons. You shook off that first goal and are looking sharp. Keep it up."

Jack and Alfie talk with their respective lines before intermission ends. When we're walking out toward a clean sheet of ice, confidence is oozing from the team.

"They're doubling up on McCord when he's out there," I point out to Jack when play resumes.

Jack nods. "Let's see if we can keep them busy enough to get the puck into the net."

"Let's tie this baby up."

It's as if putting it out there makes it happen exactly like I drew it up. McCord gets double-teamed, giving our other winger the chance to break into their zone. Their defenders realize too late he doesn't have the puck and Jessup slides it into the goal with ease.

"Way to go! Way to finish! Keep following the puck like that, boys. You're doing great."

I keep up the encouraging words as the second period turns into a battle. The Eagles keep firing away at Simmons, but he's hanging tough.

"Alright, come on. Come on," I'm muttering to myself.

Another line change and it seems the longer we skate, the faster and harder we pound away at them.

We end the second period tied, and heading into the third, the energy is high. But Edinburgh comes out firing on all cylinders.

Simmons lets in an easy goal and it amps up the Eagles. From there, it's hard for us to keep up. The guys are giving them everything they've got, but it's to no avail.

The game ends 4-2 in favor of Edinburgh.

Heads are hanging as the guys skate off the ice toward our locker room. I'm already making mental notes about where we can work in practice to improve.

"Men, that was a hard-fought game. The score might not have turned out in our favor, but I am pleased with everything I saw. You played hard all game long. Simmons, you blocked over twenty shots. From the league's top team. I want you to be proud of yourself. We'll study film, clean up some things in preparation for tomorrow's game, okay? I want an early night from all of you. No going out and getting pissed."

"Oooh, look at Coach with the slang," someone chirps.

"Alright, alright." I laugh. "Hit the showers and get cleaned up before we head out."

Even though we lost, I feel good about what I saw. We worked as a team out there. Sure, there were some sloppy passes and missed opportunities, but you can't turn one of the worst teams around overnight.

But I'm excited with our potential. About where I see this team going.

And I, for one, can't wait to share that with a certain brunette in the business department when I return on Monday.

Chapter Fifteen

TAG

"You know, I have to say I'm glad your boss is on board with you showing me around."

Liv rolls her eyes at me. Her arms are wrapped around my waist as I hold on to the strap hanging above my head. Even this time in the afternoon, the tube is packed to the brim with people.

I don't mind it one bit if it means I'm standing with Liv like this.

"Joe did say to make you feel welcome. I'm only doing as he asked."

"And it has nothing to do with you liking me?" I quirk a brow at her.

Liv holds her finger and thumb close together. "Only a little."

Grabbing her hand, I pull her toward me and seal my lips over hers. Damn. I like this woman.

A lot.

The Tube rattles to a stop, and Liv links her hand with mine as the doors open and spit us out. I follow behind her as she leads us through a maze of tunnels before the tower comes into view.

"Well, then. Since you like me only a little, does that mean this is all we're going to see?"

Liv pulls me close to her, wrapping her arm around me. With a biting wind blowing through the city, it's colder than usual. I didn't want to waste any time, so threw on the first thing I could find in my closet—a gray turtleneck sweater. Not the most comfortable, but I don't need it when I have Liv to keep me warm.

Liv, on the other hand, looks stunning, as usual. In a long camel coat, white blouse, and black pants, her long hair is flowing around her back. I like that she's not as buttoned-up as she was when we first met.

"Don't worry, I'll give you a tour of the inside too. Only since you're being good."

"If I'm really good, do I get a tour of you tonight?"

"Tag!" she hisses. A blush creeps up her cheeks that has nothing to do with the cold. "You cannot say things like that in public."

"What?" I shrug. "It's true."

Liv breaks out of my arms and walks over to the ticket booth to pick up our tickets.

We've been together a few weeks now. Between work and my travel schedule, we have to take what time together we can find. I'm thankful that we have this time when we can actually have more than just a stolen night together.

As much as I wish my focus could be all on Liv, it can't be. The team needs me. The season has been up and down. A win here, a loss there. It seems every time the guys start to get the confidence we need to take this thing down the stretch, a team comes in to rattle their determination.

"You ready?" Liv asks.

I nod, finding her hand and following her to the line. I

don't know what it is, but I love touching this woman in all the small ways.

Holding her hand.

Touching her back.

Resting my hand on her waist.

The way she sinks into my hold tells me she loves it as much as I do.

"Alright, so why is this place so historic?"

The iconic stone structure looms large as we pass over the drawbridge. The cobblestone sidewalks are uneven as people stop to take in everything before them.

"It used to be a dungeon. Prisoners—"

"Oh. I see."

"See what?" Liv questions as she leads me into an open, green courtyard. Crows are flitting about as people snap photos.

"You brought me here to leave me in the dungeons."

"Yes. That's exactly why I decided to bring you here." I can see her fighting the laugh. "Be lucky I'm not going to behead you."

"Beheadings happened here?"

She points across my body to an area across the green. "King Henry the Eighth had his second wife beheaded there."

"Seems very uncivilized of you to behead people."

"They did it to warn people from betraying their country." It's hard to listen to what she's saying because the sweet cadence of her accent is mesmerizing. "They also housed traitors here. Took them right through there."

Liv points to another area of the massive space. Tucked away in here, it's hard to hear the sounds of the city beyond.

"What do you do with traitors now?" I laugh.

"We ship them back to America."

"Something equally as uncivilized."

Liv winks at me and jogs up one of the small hills toward another smaller building. Spinning on her heel, she stops to hold out her hand for me.

An infectious smile sits on her face.

Fuck. My heart clatters around in my chest; I'm so damn happy right now. I haven't felt like this in a long time.

"I'll show you my favorite part."

"I've already seen it."

I don't need to see another thing to know that Liv is my favorite thing here. Hell, my favorite part about being in London.

"Stop it. C'mon." She waves me toward her and steers us into a line.

"What's the line for?"

"The Crown Jewels."

Once again, Liv dives into the sordid history surrounding them and where they came from.

"How is it you know so much about everything?"

The line shuffles forward and we move with them.

"I paid attention in school."

"Of course you did. Let me guess—you were always front and center answering all of the teacher's questions."

"No. I sat up front, but I did not like being called on." Liv shakes her head. "Let me guess. You were the class clown?"

"I wasn't the class clown, but the guys I usually sat with were. Means I had to study extra hard to get passing grades to stay on the hockey team."

"I always liked studying. If I didn't go into business, I think I would have made a good university professor."

We enter the building and I can see more queues of people quietly wrapped around inside.

"I don't know if I would have been a good student if I were in your class."

"Why's that?" Liv asks, crossing her arms. Almost like she's preparing herself for the answer that's coming.

"It'd be too hard to learn with a teacher so sexy."

"I knew you'd say that."

I lean down and press a kiss to the corner of her mouth. "Glad I'm predictable."

Liv continues to shower me with facts about the immense place we're visiting as we weave our way through the lines—both the good and the not so favorable. I could listen to her talk all day about anything and everything.

When did I become so taken with her?

"Oh, look. We're here!"

The excitement oozes from her as we step onto the moving walkway in the dark room. Overhead lights illuminate a row of glass display cases.

Crowns with deep purple velvet.

Scepters encrusted with diamonds.

Necklaces with gleaming sapphires.

Rings with sparkling rubies.

"Aren't they gorgeous?"

I drop my chin to her shoulder as we pass by. "Are you hinting that you want me to steal these for you?"

"Tag!" She elbows me in the stomach. "Don't joke about that."

"Or what? Will they throw me in the dungeons?"

"If you get arrested, I am not coming to visit you."

I laugh as our turn ends and we end up in a gift shop filled with trinkets from the tower. "I see where I stand."

"Poor you."

We head into the now dull gray afternoon and wander the grounds. It's the perfect way to spend the day. Clouds start to move in, threatening rain.

"You know what could be a good way to pass the time?" I ask.

"What's that?"

"Maybe we could go climb the bridge? If you're okay with it."

Liv glances at her watch. "It closes soon."

Linking my hand with hers, I lead us to the exit. "Let's see if we can do it, okay?"

She smiles back at me. "Lead the way."

Chapter Sixteen

OLIVIA

By the time we make it to the Tower Bridge, a light rain patters down around us. The roads are slick as cars whiz by.

People are hurrying into pubs to wait out the weather.

"Wait here."

Tag hurries towards the ticket booth as I stand under an awning to try and stay dry. The skies are darkening fast as the rain picks up. A river cruise sails under the bridge with very few people on the open deck. I breathe in the cold air, letting it fill my lungs. My phone buzzes in my pocket. I half expect it to be from Imogen or Sienna, inviting me out tonight, but it's not.

DAD

> Your mother said that you are still working for the hockey team. If you would like me to enquire about more suitable positions for you in the city, please email my secretary and she will work on this

Of course.

There should be no point in getting worked up over a text, but it's hard not to. I haven't spoken to either of my parents since the day in the park, but what I do get is another reminder that I am not living up to the Montrose name.

All they want is for their daughter to have a suitable job and a man they deem appropriate.

"You ready?"

"What?" I spin, stuffing my phone into my coat pocket.

"Let's go." Tag holds the door open for me, waving two tickets in hand.

"Isn't it closing?" I ask, following him inside.

The sexy man in front of me beams back at me. "I paid him off. We get it for another two hours."

"Really?"

He nods. "No one is here because of the weather, so really, they're making money off us."

Linking his hand with mine, Tag pulls me toward the exhibit entrance. Wide, chocolate-brown stairs disappear up through the maze of the tower. On the first landing, there's the history of the bridge and its construction.

It's quiet. I guess the man working was right when he said no one was coming here today.

Tag isn't bothering to stop and read about the history as we pass. By the time we make it to the walkways over the roadway below, my breathing is labored.

"Okay, not all of us are training with the hockey team every day, Tag," I tell him.

Plexiglass lets us see everything below us. Lights flash up from cars and buses passing on the road.

"Does being this high bother you?" Tag asks, walking

towards the middle of the walkway. "It seems weird that we can see straight down."

"I don't like heights, but this doesn't bother me."

"Really?" Tag glances at me before coming over to take my hand. "I was wondering why you agreed to this."

It's quiet up here with no one else with us. The lights of the city flicker through the low clouds.

Walking towards the middle of the bridge, I rest my hands on the railing in front of the glass windows. "This bridge has been here for so long, that it feels unmovable. Like when I'm up here, nothing is going to happen to me."

"Really?" Tag moves behind me, wrapping his arms around my waist.

I sink back into his touch, reveling in his warmth, nodding. "I feel safe with all the metal. I know it seems counterintuitive, but it's like it's holding me up."

Tag sweeps my hair to the side and presses a kiss to my neck. Heat snakes through me at the soft touch.

"You're pretty incredible, you know that?"

"Not really."

"Yes, you are." His voice is firm. Strong hands drift low on my waist, untucking the blouse. "Let me show you just how incredible you are."

Tag's hand pushes into my pants. The callouses on his hands cause goose pimples to erupt all over my skin.

"Tag, we can't." It's not much of a protest. In fact, I push back into him, urging him on.

"Why not? There's no one here but us." His hand dips lower, finding the hem of my panties and brushing past them. "Let go, Liv. You're safe with me."

Grasping onto his forearm, I push his hand down farther. "Do it."

"That's it, baby."

Tag sinks one finger inside me, and it takes everything I have not to come immediately.

I wrap the side of my coat around my front to hide what we're doing.

"Do you think all those people on the boats down there can see what we're doing?" Tag's voice is a whisper. "See that I'm going to make you come on my hand while we're standing here and they're gazing around at all the sights?"

"Make me come," I beg.

Pressure builds as I sink my nails into Tag's forearm, urging him on. Wanting him to go deeper.

"I love how needy you are for me. That you didn't even question as I finger this sweet little pussy of yours."

I tip my head back onto his shoulder as his breath ghosts across my cheek. "So needy. So needy for you, Tag."

"Are you imagining it's my cock? That I'm bending you over and fucking you from behind?"

"Gah! I want that."

"How badly?" Tag nips at my ear. "Because if you don't come for me like the good little girl I know you are, you won't get my cock."

He pushes two fingers inside of me, and I grind down on his hand. I don't care where we are. I don't care that anyone could happen upon us.

All I want is to come undone in this man's arms. His hard length presses into my hip as I rock against him.

"I'm so close."

Tag tilts my chin towards him and captures my mouth in a searing kiss. Between his tongue and fingers, I erupt.

Stars explode behind my eyes as he swallows down my moans of delight. I hold on tight, because if not, I might float off into the abyss.

"Fuck, Liv. Fuck!" Tag's shouts are muffled as the most perfect orgasm washes over me.

"Tag…did you?" I trail off as he buries his face in my neck.

"Yup. I fucking came. Because you are so God damn hard to resist, I couldn't contain myself."

He slips his hand out, allowing me to spin in his arms. Grasping his sweater, I pull him in for a kiss. It's slow and sweet. Heated and passionate all at the same time.

"Well then. We better get home because we need to take care of this little problem."

Tag grins down at me. "Not a problem because seeing you lose control and let go like that with me? I'll never say no to it."

"Then let's go."

From: Stanley Easton III <seaston@londonlight-
ning.co.uk>
Sent: Wednesday, November 12, 2025 9:32 AM
To: Olivia Montrose <omontrose@londonlightning.co.uk>
Subject: Thank You

Miss Montrose,

I wanted to thank you for taking me out and seeing the
sights of London. Having been focused on hockey, I have
not had the chance to see the city and appreciate you
taking time out of your busy schedule to do so.

Thanks,
Stanley Easton III
Head Coach - London Lightning

From: Olivia Montrose <omontrose@londonlight-
ning.co.uk>
Sent: Wednesday, November 12, 2025 9:33 AM
To: Stanley Easton III <seaston@londonlightning.co.uk>
Subject: RE: Thank You

Mr. Easton,

Why are you bringing attention to the fact that I showed
you the city?

Regards,

Olivia Montrose
Business Department
London Lightning

From: Stanley Easton III <seaston@londonlight-
ning.co.uk>
Sent: Wednesday, November 12, 2025 9:52 AM
To: Olivia Montrose <omontrose@londonlightning.co.uk>
Subject: RE: Thank You

Miss Montrose,

Only thanking one of the hardest working employees the
Lightning has. Keeping it professional ;)

Thanks,
Stanley Easton III
Head Coach - London Lightning

From: Olivia Montrose <omontrose@londonlight-
ning.co.uk>
Sent: Wednesday, November 12, 2025 10:18 AM
To: Stanley Easton III <seaston@londonlightning.co.uk>
Subject: RE: Thank You

Mr. Easton,

Please consider any future travel plans cancelled in order to
remain professional.

Regards,

Olivia Montrose
Business Department
London Lightning

From: Stanley Easton III <seaston@londonlight-
ning.co.uk>

Sent: Wednesday, November 12, 2025 10:21 AM
To: Olivia Montrose <omontrose@londonlightning.co.uk>
Subject: RE: Thank You

Miss Montrose,

I'll be very happy to keep it professional in any one of London's many other beautiful sights ;)

Thanks,
Stanley Easton III
Head Coach - London Lightning

From: Olivia Montrose <omontrose@londonlight-ning.co.uk>
Sent: Wednesday, November 12, 2025 10:27 AM
To: Stanley Easton III <seaston@londonlightning.co.uk>
Subject: RE: Thank You

I hate you.

From: Stanley Easton III <seaston@londonlight-ning.co.uk>
Sent: Wednesday, November 12, 2025 10:31 AM
To: Olivia Montrose <omontrose@londonlightning.co.uk>
Subject: RE: Thank You

No, you don't. Way to be professional, Liv.

Thanks,
Stanley Easton III
Head Coach - London Lightning

Chapter Seventeen

TAG

"I think you have an ulterior motive for bringing me to a museum today, Liv."

"Mmm, and what motive might that be?"

We pass through the ticket turnstile as our tickets get scanned. "I think you want to make sure things stay PG today."

A blush stains her cheeks as we walk into the main room of the museum. A soaring, glass-domed ceiling greets us. Shadows spill across the marble floor. Long, stone columns grace each wall, leading to different areas of the building.

"As enjoyable as that was, Tag," Liv tells me, "you cannot rent out this museum for us to do that again."

"I could ask."

"Stop." Liv grabs my hand and leads me through one of the archways. Wood, herringbone floors echo beneath our feet. "I love this place and want to show you more of my favorite things. Besides, we can't be outside in the rain."

If I had to show her everything I loved in here, it would be a short tour.

Her. Just Liv.

The thought slams into me out of nowhere.

Damn. In the few short months I've been here, I've fallen for Liv. This woman who is my opposite in every way.

Quiet and shy where I'm loud and never meet a stranger.

More than ten years my junior.

Someone who pushes back at me every chance she gets.

I love this woman. Every side she shows me. The daring side. The reserved side. Every little piece of her, I love.

"This way."

She guides me down another hallway, darker than the previous one. There's no windows here. The only light comes from the small bulbs casting their glow from the bottom of the floor.

Liv stops in front of an old painting with a gold frame. "This is one of my favorites."

Bursts of golden yellow—sunflowers—are painted across the canvas. Some are wilting, while others don't have any petals on them at all. It's not the best thing I've ever seen, but art isn't something I've ever taken an interest in.

Liv? I have a vested interest in her.

"Tell me why this is your favorite."

Liv studies the painting, crossing her arms as she stares it, teeth worrying her bottom lip. "I don't know. It always felt hopeful to me."

"Hopeful? Hopeful about what?"

Aside from a few comments about her parents, I haven't gotten much out of her about her past.

"It felt like sunshine when things got to be too much."

"What was too much?" I step behind her, letting her know I'm there with my presence. For once, I don't touch her. It seems if I do, she might shut down on me.

"The weight of being perfect," she confesses.

"Who says you have to be perfect?"

"It always felt like there was an immense weight that I had to be perfect. Not a hair out of place. Not a paper that didn't receive perfect marks. A piano recital practiced to perfection."

"Really?"

Liv tilts her head to look at me before looking back at the painting. "Growing up wasn't easy for me. If I wanted my parents' attention, I had to be perfect. Anything less than that, and I wouldn't get it."

"I'm sorry." I don't know what else I can tell her. "Are you close with your parents?"

She shakes her head as she moves on to another painting. "Not as close as I want to be."

Her shoulders hang heavy with her confession as she moves down the dark hall. Fuck. I hate that anyone would ever make this woman feel an ounce of pain. Liv is probably the most perfect person on the planet, and she doesn't even have to try. At least not in my book.

"This is another one of my favorites."

We stop in front of an old painting of a table with people surrounding it. Fruit is heaped on the table.

Breads.

Wine.

It looks like a party of sorts. Having just heard her confession earlier, I can see why she likes this one. Love and happiness ooze from the painting. The sweet woman I love yearned for something she never got from the people that were supposed to love her unconditionally.

"Do you come here often?" I ask her.

"Not as often anymore. When I moved here for uni, I came all the time. It's an easy place to get lost."

Clutching her by the shoulder, I take her into my arms. She clings to me as we stand in this dark hallway with people moving around us.

"If you ever get lost again, find me. I won't let that happen. Ever."

She squeezes me tighter. Nothing else needs to be said. I would do anything to protect the woman in my arms. She is precious in every way.

Would I feel this way about her if we hadn't met that first weekend in London? I don't know, but I am so fucking thankful that Alfie invited me out.

"Thanks for bringing me here today." I press a kiss to the crown of her head.

She rests her chin on my chest, looking up at me. "I mean, there's not much else we could have done."

"Is it going to be nothing but rainy days from here until the spring?"

Liv laughs and I kiss her forehead. Good. I don't want to see this woman sad for even a second.

"Yes. Better get used to it now."

The rest of the afternoon goes by without incident. Liv is more subdued, but still gives me a tour that is better than anything else I would find here. By the time we're standing outside under the massive entryway, it's pouring.

Before I can dart out into the rain to find a black taxi, she stops me. "Thank you for listening today, Tag."

"Always. I'm here for you, whatever you need."

The rose perfume she wears infiltrates my senses and threatens to overwhelm me. I don't want to scare her away with my feelings for her. Now is not the right time to tell her. Not when she's so vulnerable.

"Why don't we stop into one of the pubs and grab a bite before we go back to my flat?" I ask her.

"You like these pubs here, don't you?"

"It brought me you, didn't it?"

Chapter Eighteen

OLIVIA

I pick at a loose string on my gloves. Winter has settled in the city, and while I could wait for Tag inside, I don't want to miss him. The date night I have planned is something so unlike me, I don't know how I came up with it.

Well, I do know.

Imogen was talking about doing it with her newest boy toy, and well, why not?

After the heaviness of my confession to Tag about my parents, I wanted to get things back on track.

Things are supposed to be fun, not heavy. Heavy leads to more feelings, and more feelings lead to things going off plan.

"Hey, baby."

Tag's sultry voice as he walks towards me pulls me from my thoughts.

"Wow."

He certainly got the dress code right. He didn't balk at all when I told him he needed to dress nicer for the evening.

Not that he doesn't look sexy at all times, but with the

buttoned-up shirt, tie, and sport coat, he looks positively dreamy.

"You clean up nicely," I tell him, tugging him close by the strap of his overnight bag crossed over his chest.

"It's a shame I can't see what's under this coat."

The black coat reaches my knees, hiding the slinky dress underneath. I'm in my least sensible pair of heels for the evening.

"You'll see it soon enough."

Pecking his cheek, I hold my hand out to hail a taxi.

"Still no hint of where this epic date is that you're taking me on?"

Tag opens the door to the taxi, and I step inside, giving the driver the address.

"Don't you want to be surprised?"

His hand rests on my knee as the driver pulls away into the evening. I rest my hand over his, dragging my fingers along the veins in his hand.

Tag leans over and nips at my ear. "I don't care what we do, as long as I'm doing it with you."

Cupping his cheek, I pull his mouth towards mine and kiss him. I don't care that we're in the back of a dark taxi. I need his touch more than anything.

It's a scary thought, but the moment his tongue touches mine, every thought flies from my head.

All I want is Tag.

Heat swirls around us as desire takes root in my chest. I arch into his touch as he swallows my quiet gasps.

Something I've learned about Tag is he is an excellent kisser. Soft. Firm. Controlled.

I've never experienced anything like it.

"Here."

I'm in a daze as I pull back, staring at his lust-filled eyes.

"Want to say fuck it to the evening and head home?" Tag asks, tucking a lock of hair behind my ear.

I shake my head, pulling out the fare to pay the cab driver. "No."

He groans next to me. "Fine."

"Trust me. You'll enjoy this evening."

"And where exactly is this evening taking place?" A row of townhouses is stretched out before us as we step onto the sidewalk. "Are you going to harvest my organs?"

I swat at his chest as I find the correct house. It's white stone with a black door and a light shining out the front window.

"There will be none of that this evening," I tell him, linking hands and dragging him towards the door. "Not that I would have the pertinent skills to do that."

"That's the only thing that is stopping you?"

Tag laughs as I knock on the door. The door opens to reveal a woman dressed in a black silk robe. Her dark hair is slicked back in a low bun and her face is expertly made up.

"You must be Miss Montrose."

"Hi there."

"Welcome, welcome." She sweeps us into the entryway. "Welcome to the Lust Supper."

The door clicks shut behind us as Tag crowds behind me.

"Did I hear her correctly?" he whispers.

"Please, follow me. My name is Wendy and I will be your host this evening."

I don't reply as I follow her up two sets of stairs. The walls are bare, nothing but paint coating them. On the second floor, a small table sits holding a single lamp and mirror. We're led to another room right off the landing.

"This will be your room for the evening. Once you're

ready, dinner will be served across the hall. It will be ready whenever you are, and once finished, you may return to your room for the rest of the evening. As a reminder, the rooms are soundproof, so you can be as loud or as quiet as you like."

With a wink, she bows her way out of the room and the two of us are left alone.

The lamps are dim, covered in red silk, casting romantic shadows across the room. The large bed is covered in rose petals, and a bottle of champagne rests in a silver bucket on the dresser.

"Okay, what is this 'Lust Supper?'" Tag asks, crossing his arms and leaning against the wall.

The look he fixes me with has me squeezing my legs together.

"Exactly what it sounds like. We enjoy a sexy meal together, a couples massage if we want one, and then we get to spend the night here."

Tag stalks towards me like I'm the prey he is going to devour. His fingers find the buttons on my coat and unfasten them. His eyes widen as he pushes the soft material over my shoulders.

"Damn, Liv. This might be the best surprise of all."

The strapless red dress dips between my breasts. It is ruched on the sides and hits mid-thigh. It's simple, but it has the intended effect as Tag runs his hands over me.

"Do you like it?"

"Fuck, yes. I can't wait to peel you out of it after dinner."

I rest my hands on his chest. "I can't wait to peel *you* out of this."

Tag groans, burying his face in my neck. "Are you sure we have to go to dinner?"

I pull back, taking his hands in mine and backing out of the room. "Yes. Because we'll need our energy."

"Oh yeah?" The look on his face is downright sinful.

"C'mon. The faster we eat, the faster we can get back in here."

He crowds behind me as we walk into the other room. Heavy, velvet curtains cover the windows. Soft music plays from a speaker. Candles dripping wax sit on the table.

"You outdid yourself on this, Liv."

Tag helps me into my seat as Wendy appears with a tray of food.

"Feel free to take your time. Oysters. A pasta dish with a chili sauce. Chocolate dipped strawberries, and figs to finish off the meal. And," she flourishes her arm, "red wine for both. Bon appétit."

Wendy disappears, leaving the two of us together, sitting side by side. Tag grabs his glass and holds it up.

"Cheers to a sexy evening, Olivia."

"Cheers, Stanley."

I clink my glass to his before taking a sip of the robust drink, then I pick up an oyster with the tiny fork.

"I had no idea you had something like this in you."

Stabbing the meat, I hold it out to Tag. "I guess I'm full of surprises."

The way his lips close over the tines has my body shuddering. Heat bursts in his dark eyes as he licks his lips.

"Delicious." He takes the fork from me and gets my own bite ready for me. "Your turn."

The entire meal is like this. Feeding one another. Staring into each other's eyes.

My need for the man sitting across from me is at an all-time high. Being here in this small room, eating these sensual foods, is turning me on in a way I've never felt before.

I'm drunk on lust for Tag. By the time he holds a strawberry out for me to eat, I'm ready to throw him down on the table and have my way with him. I close my lips around his fingers, dragging my tongue over them.

I have never felt so wanton in my life.

And we haven't even gotten to the last surprise sitting in my bag.

Wendy knocks on the door, peeking her head inside. "Shall we start the massages?"

"You know what, Wendy? I think we'll pass," Tag says, not looking at her.

"They are included," she clarifies.

My nipples pebble under his stare. I don't want a couples massage. All I want is to be with Tag.

Something that we both seem to be in agreement on. His tone leaves no room for argument.

"Not tonight."

Chapter Nineteen

TAG

Fuck. Me.

I have never been so hard in my entire God damn life. From the minute we walked into the small suite and Liv shucked her coat, I've been dying to sink inside her sweet pussy.

A Lust Supper?

I had no idea such a thing existed.

It was an exercise in patience as Liv and I touched and fed each other during dinner. All I wanted to do was pull her into my lap and fuck her senseless.

Walking back into the room, I kick the door shut and start to undo the buttons on my shirt.

"Care to help?" Liv pulls her hair over one shoulder and turns away from me.

"Gladly."

The sound of the zipper snicks through the room as I pull it lower, over the curve of her ass. Grabbing the sides of the material, I help her out of it. It pools into a pile by her feet.

"Holy shit," I mutter to myself.

Liv turns, in nothing but her fuck-me heels and a lacy black thong.

"You like?"

"Olivia." I wrap my hands around her waist and pull her close. "You look stunning."

"Thank you." She steals a kiss before gliding her hands over my still-covered abs. "Now, time for you to strip."

She doesn't have to tell me twice. I undo the buckle on my belt and shed my shoes, socks, and pants before pulling my shirt off.

Liv stops my hand before I can take off my briefs.

"Hold on. I have one more surprise for you." Liv grabs her purse and pulls out a black, felt bag.

"What's that?" I rub a hand over my hard dick through my briefs, not sure if I'm going to make it much longer.

"Open it." Liv tosses it my way and I catch it with ease.

Pulling the drawstrings open, I'm stunned. "Really?"

Liv steps toward me and I instinctively wrap a hand around her. Her skin is so damn soft. Nipples diamond hard as they brush against my chest.

"I thought they would be fun to try tonight."

"A cock ring and rope? Liv…I don't know what to say."

"Say yes."

"Yes. Fuck, yes."

Fusing our mouths together, I pour every bit of excitement for what the night holds into this kiss.

Her body melts into mine as I deepen our connection. Every nerve ending of mine is on fire as her hands slide down my chest.

"Before we start, we need a safe word," I tell her as she pushes me back.

"Bridge."

A lopsided smile pulls the corner of my mouth. "Seems you already thought of this."

Liv moves back toward the bed. "You could say that. Now, let's get started."

"Then get on the bed," I command. "And leave the heels on."

Tossing the bag on the bed, complete with a strip of condoms, I grab the rope in my hand. The thought of tying Liv up and having my way with her has the tip of my cock peeking out of my briefs.

"Looks like someone is ready to join the party."

"We'll get there. Now, get on your back with your hands above your head."

"What do you plan on doing?"

Liv sits in the middle of the bed, but doesn't lie down.

Oh, this is going to be fun.

"First, I'm going to tie you up. Then I'm going to fuck that pretty little mouth of yours. After that, well, I might eat your pussy before I put on this ring and fuck us both into oblivion."

"I want it all."

I rid myself of my briefs and watch as her eyes go to my dick. "Then why don't you be a good little girl and do as I ask, hmm?"

Once she is lying on her back, I grab Liv's wrists and tie them together before securing them on a loose slat in the headboard. Perfect design for something like this.

"You are so fucking sexy, Liv." I drag a lone finger from her chin, down her neck, over her nipples, and back up. "I love how you react to me."

Her body writhes beneath me as I move over her. "I'm so wet, Tag."

Brushing her thong to the side, I sink two fingers inside her. "Yeah you are."

I move in and out of her at a lazy pace, soaking my fingers before pulling them out.

"Why'd you stop?" she whines.

"Like I said—I'm going to fuck your mouth before anything else." Her eyes travel down my body as I give myself a lazy stroke, lubricating myself with her wetness. "What's the safe word again?"

She smiles up at me. "Bridge."

"Good girl."

Straddling her chest, I brush the head of my leaking cock over her lips. She opens at first taste.

Slipping inside her warm, wet mouth, it takes everything I have not to come immediately.

Feeding this woman my cock? It's a sight that will forever be burned into my memory.

"Do you know how good you look sucking me down?" I bump the back of her throat. Pulling back then pushing back in, I watch as she takes me with a hunger I've never seen.

It's like being at this place has given her permission to be a different Olivia entirely.

Her mouth is full, lips stretched wide around me as precum and spit gather at the corners. Her moans vibrate around me as I keep pushing in and out of her mouth.

"Fuck. I'm going to come. Do you want it?"

She gives me the briefest nod and I smile at her. Threading a hand through her hair, I hold her head still as I thrust in and out. It doesn't take more than a few pumps before I'm coming down her throat.

Liv squirms beneath me as her eyes shut, drinking down everything I'm giving her.

Once she's completely drained me, I pull out. My cock is still semi-hard. A testament to how this woman makes me feel.

"Do you know how sexy you look right now?" I wipe

the corner of her mouth with my thumb, pushing it into her mouth to suck it off.

"I want more," she tells me. "I want you to make me come again."

"Again?" Shifting down the bed, I push her legs apart. I can smell the sweet scent of her release. "Did you come when I did?"

She nods. "Yes. It felt so good."

"Well." I throw her legs over my shoulders and bury my face in her pussy. "I'm going to make you feel even better."

"Tag!" Liv shouts.

I love how unburdened she is as I strum her clit with my tongue. Liv is completely gone tonight. No sense of decorum in sight. She looks thoroughly fucked and I haven't even gotten my dick inside of her.

Her shouts spur me on. Her thighs squeeze my head as I drink up the wetness that leaks out of her.

Fuck. I have never seen her this turned on before. She's a squirming mess as I continue my assault on her pussy. It's my favorite thing, making her feel like this.

When she's coming again on my tongue, my dick is rock hard and I'm ready for another round.

"Fucking delicious." I wipe my mouth as her body goes limp under mine. A lazy smile sits on her lips. "You think you can go another round?"

She tries to sit up, but the ropes stop her. She looks annoyed, but turns her gaze to mine. "If you stop now, Tag, I will never forgive you."

I push her back down onto the bed and cover her with my weight. "You know we have all night, right?"

"Which means more chances for more sex. But I want to come on your cock."

Said cock in question stirs. "Say that again."

"That I want to come on your cock?"

"Yes."

A devious smile locks into place. "I want to come on your cock, Tag. Do it. Fuck me."

I sit back on my heels and find the black bag. "You know egging me on isn't going to get you what you want."

She sighs. "Well, I've already had two orgasms. I guess I can wait."

"Can you?" I brush my thumb over her clit.

"Yes," she moans.

"Right. So I guess I'll just sit here and play with this myself?"

I twirl the ring around on my finger.

"Ugh. Fine. Hurry up. I want to come again."

"Knew it, my greedy little girl."

Turning on the ring, I slather it in lube with the small packet given and roll it down my cock.

Nothing like a vibrating cock ring to get you completely hard again.

"Fuck. This might be something we need to play with more."

"Let me feel it."

"Patience, baby." I nip at her neck, sucking at the spot to mark her. "Let me suit up."

Tearing open the condom packet, I roll it over my cock. Ripples of anticipation roll off Liv.

"Tag!" she shouts as I push inside her in one go.

Her breasts bounce as I thrust in and out of her. My hips piston at a quick pace. Both of us are already at the edge, having come once—or in her case, twice—before.

I jack my hips. I'm unrelenting as Liv pulls at her bindings. Her shouts spur me on. Her pussy chokes my dick every time I bottom out.

"You feel so damn good, baby. So perfect. Like your pussy was made for my cock."

"Yes. I love the way you make me feel."

Dragging my cock out, I thrust a few more times before she comes again. I bury my face in her neck, licking and sucking on her pulsing vein as my own release snakes through me.

Fuck. It's overwhelming as I try to calm the riot of emotions swimming through me. It's more than just lust and desire. It's love for this woman who gave so much of herself to me tonight.

I don't deserve this woman.

Slipping out of her, I remove the condom, tie it off, and dump it into the wastebin. I release the ropes, rubbing the red marks on her wrists.

Our breathing evens out as we lie together in each other's arms.

"How are you feeling?" I whisper, holding her close, checking in with her.

"Perfect. Absolutely perfect. You?"

"Perfect. Absolutely perfect."

Chapter Twenty

TAG

"Where are you taking me?"

"Relax, Liv. You'll like it."

"You know I don't like surprises."

Drawing to a stop at the crosswalk, I wrap my arms around Liv's hips. "I know. It's not like I'm taking you to some sex club."

"Sex club?" She quirks a brow at me. "Really, Tag?"

Leaning down, I kiss just below her ear, feeling the reaction it gets. "You've already taken us to one."

"Tag!" she hisses. "It was not a sex club."

"It was pretty sexy to me."

"My point still stands." Liv looks both ways before pressing up onto her toes and whispering in my ear, "It was not a sex club."

"Well, sadly, we are going to a bar."

The light turns and I check both ways—still not quite sure which way to look—and cross the road.

"A bar is good."

"Not just a bar." I waggle my eyebrows at her. "A game bar."

"Is there a game on tonight?"

Even from here, I can see her thinking.

"Not that kind of game. We're going to play some games."

"Really?"

Spotting the entrance, I hold open the door for Liv. "Really. Hope you brought your A game."

The bar is loud as I grab hold of Liv's hand and pull her through the crowds. Tables are spread out with people playing beer pong. A stage is set up on the other side with a karaoke machine. People crowd the bar in the back, waiting on drinks.

"What are we playing tonight?" Liv asks.

"You keep showing me your favorite things and taking me around the city, so I thought it might be nice to do something I like and play some Ping-Pong."

"Have you not been enjoying yourself?" She completely ignores the answer to her previous question.

Liv loves her questions.

"Do you know how fucking cute you are?" Grasping her chin, I turn her focus to me. "Of course I've been enjoying myself. More than enjoying, actually. But I wanted to take you out tonight and not have you worry about planning."

"You know I do enjoy making plans."

"Well, tonight, I'm in charge."

Liv rests her hands on my chest. "Are you now?"

"Damn straight I am. Now, how about I get us some drinks and we start playing?"

"Gin and ginger beer, please."

I steal a swift kiss. "As if I don't know that."

I know everything about Liv. She is my favorite person in this city. Hell, the world at this point.

Ordering our drinks, I keep my eyes on her. I can't help

myself. She's in a simple black sweater, dark jeans, and black ankle booties, but she looks sexy as sin.

I don't know if Liv would have given me the time of day if we hadn't already met before we met in an *official* capacity at work. She's too polished and buttoned-up for that.

Even if it's not against the rules.

"Here you go." Drinks are dropped off in front of me and I pull out a few notes to cover them.

"Thanks, mate."

"Cheers."

Weaving my way through the crowd, I find Liv perched on a barstool near the back wall. Her eyes are bouncing around as she takes in the place. Based on how wide her eyes are, I'm guessing she's never been here before.

"Is this place not your usual haunt?" I ask, startling her.

"I think you know the answer to that. I don't have a sporting bone in my body."

"I think there's a bad joke in there somewhere." I laugh.

Liv groans before taking a sip of her drink, smacking her lips together. "You know, sometimes I forget how much older than me you are until you say things like that."

"Hey, I didn't actually say it. You're the one who said it."

"And I regret it." Liv hops down off the stool. "Now, why don't we get started on Ping-Pong."

Resting a hand on her hip, I guide her through the crowds toward the table I reserved for us.

"You know, I don't think I have ever played Ping-Pong before," Liv tells me.

"You haven't? Not even as a kid?"

Two paddles and a handful of plastic balls are resting in the container that hangs from the table.

"It was more dinners with my father's colleagues and sitting quietly or playing the piano to impress them."

"No skinned knees from playing outside?"

"No." She shakes her head. "Now, are we going to play or what?"

"For someone who's never played, you sound pretty cocky there, Liv."

Taking a sip of her drink, she sets it down on the ledge next to the table. "Maybe I have a hidden talent of kicking your arse at Ping-Pong."

"Wow. The trash talk starts." I set my own drink next to hers and take the paddle she hands me. "I'll have you know, I'm fairly good at Ping-Pong."

She rolls her eyes as we each move to an end of the table. "Considering you were a great hockey player, I'd assume you have a natural talent for sports."

That stops me from serving the ball over the net. "And how do you know I was a great hockey player?"

I've talked about playing with her, but more in generalities. It's not like I was part of a winning team. I loved my team, but yeah…we sucked.

She looks sheepish. "I may or may not have looked up your career highlights."

Setting the paddle down, I walk around the table and pull Liv into me. "Why Miss Montrose, who knew you were into hockey players."

"Retired hockey players." She pokes my chest. "And I'm rethinking my feelings for them at the moment."

I lean down, kissing the corner of her mouth. "It's okay to admit you like me."

From Liv? That's practically a confession of love. But I don't let myself think that far ahead.

"I'll admit no such thing."

An idea comes to mind. "If I win, will you tell me?"

"Now who's getting cocky?"

"Considering you just told me that you've never played, I like the odds."

Liv pushes me back around to my side of the table and I start the game. The ball bounces on her side of the table and she goes to hit it, but whiffs.

"Oh." She looks behind her to where the ball landed. "I guess this might not be as easy as I thought."

"Try serving to me."

This time, she's able to do it, but the minute I send it back to her, it's another miss. The look of confusion on her face as she tries to hit it is fucking adorable.

We go back and forth. I score most of the points with Liv getting more annoyed with each miss or errant shot she hits.

"Let me try serving again." Liv finishes her drink as I toss the ball to her. "I want to get at least one point off a serve."

"Good luck." I wink at her.

She rolls her eyes at me as she hits the ball onto my side. I make a half-hearted attempt to hit it and let it glance over my paddle.

Except, I don't do as good of a job as I thought because Liv is marching around the table, stabbing her paddle at me.

"I don't want your pity points!" she huffs in protest. "I want a point the right way."

"I wasn't giving you a pity point." I throw my hands up in defense. "I missed."

"You missed on purpose."

"And if I did?"

Her eyes light up as she sets the paddle down on the

table. "Then I am not going to give you what you want when you win."

Snaking a hand around her waist, I tug her close. "You realize by telling me that you *won't* tell me that, you're actually telling me it?"

"Wait, what? Now you've confused me."

My lips ghost the shell of her ear. "You just told me you like me."

"I did…oh. I suppose I did."

Her body relaxes, sinking into my hold.

"I guess I can tell you that I like you too."

"Good," she replies. "I guess I like you even if you're trying to let me win."

"Oh, no." I pull back. "I was giving you a point. You would kill me if I let you win."

"I would." She looks satisfied at that. "Now, how about another round? Whoever wins gets to choose where we have sex first."

This time, there is no pretense in letting her win or get points.

I have never won a game faster.

Chapter Twenty-One

TAG

"Tell me you're going to watch the game tonight?" I question Liv.

The bus pulls out from the hotel as I relax into the seat while on the phone with Liv before heading to the rink.

A place I can honestly say I've never been? Wales. They have a decent team. I've been studying a lot of film. They've got a good defensive pair, but their offensive line could use some work.

"The girls are coming over and we're going to stream it on the television."

I smile at her words. "Good. I have a feeling it's going to be a good night."

"And maybe if you keep winning, the game will become more popular here and will be on TV."

"Liv, I don't know if that's going to happen. Football is too popular here."

Something I've come to terms with.

I can hear her smile over the phone, if that is such a thing. "I know you're going to turn the Lightning into the world's best team and bring all sorts of new fans to the game. Then it'll be too big to ignore."

"I feel like that's both a compliment and a dig all at the same time."

Liv laughs, warm and silky. The perfect sound on this cold, Welsh evening. "Expectations, Stanley. You have to know where you stand with football. But you'll get there."

"You say the sweetest things."

"It's a good thing you like me."

"I know. Listen, have fun with the girls. I'll see you tomorrow night when we get back, yeah?"

"Good luck."

The ride to the rink is short, and as I'm hanging up, we're pulling in. The team is excited. We've been working all week toward this matchup. With one of their starting wingers out with a torn MCL, it's opened up the game tonight.

One that I hope we can win.

Going through our usual pregame warm-ups, I reiterate to the guys everything we've discussed in practice. How we're a great team and can go out there and compete with them.

It's a simple thing, but the more I say it, the more they seem to believe it. I don't know much about their old coach or how he led, but I don't think he was the most encouraging of the guys.

By the time the puck drops, we're brimming with energy. Passes are executed well. Simmons is defending the net like he was made to be there. And McCord gets an easy shot on goal that puts a point on the board.

"It's nice to see all of their hard work paying off," Jack tells me.

He looks extra sharp tonight in a dark gray suit with

blue tie. It matches the team colors. Better than the usual suit he wears.

I wonder why.

"They've got the skills. They just needed someone to believe in them."

Wales makes a sloppy pass that Jessup capitalizes on and goes flying down the ice. It earns us another point.

"Way to finish. Great job reading the plays. Keep it up."

When the puck drops again, Wales nabs it and takes off. Simmons gets low and does a great job defending the goal.

"Hell, yeah!" I cheer from the bench. He can't hear me from the boos in the crowd, but I'm proud of him. He's worked hard on improving his skills this season. And watching as he again defends the net when they fire the puck off, he plucks it out of the air with his glove.

The horn sounds for the end of the first period, and we're up 2-0. I whistle, following the guys down toward our locker room.

"What a great first period, men!" I clap, shouting around the room. It echoes in the concrete space. "We're looking good out there. Working as a team. Helping each other move the puck down the ice. Simmons, you're doing a great job. Let's keep it up, okay?

"Yes, Coach," they fire back at me.

They heed my advice as we head back out for the second period. Even if we don't score, they keep Wales from scoring.

"We're really looking good," Alfie says.

"Must be all that practice," Jack deadpans.

I laugh at the two of them as the guys hop over the boards for a line change.

This is fun. This is why I love hockey. Now that we're

winning, the guys are enjoying themselves more and more. It's amazing what a few wins can do to boost a team's confidence.

And by the time the final whistle blows, we've won 5-2, scoring an easy empty net goal.

I shake hands with their coach before heading back to the locker room. My first thought is whether Liv will be impressed. A win is a win, but I don't think it'll get us any closer to being the most popular sport here.

At least according to her.

God, I really do love her. Even if she insults my sport.

Chapter Twenty-Two

OLIVIA

"This is what you had in mind for tonight?"

I tug at the hem of Tag's sweatshirt I'm wearing. "I figured if we're doing new and adventurous things, I might as well conquer some fears. And you can see more of London."

"On a slide?" he asks.

"Yes."

After another missed connection with my parents this afternoon, I was frustrated. Tag sensed it and suggested we go out.

I didn't tell him the real reason I was upset. I don't want to give my parents any more power over me than necessary.

This time, the telephone barely rang before I was being sent to voicemail. What parents send their daughter to voicemail?

Short of surprising them with a visit to get them to talk to me, I'm not sure what else I can do.

So instead of dinner at the pub, I figured we could go for something more adventurous.

"Not exactly what I thought we'd be doing tonight."

"Are you scared?" I ask, staring up at the red metal that shoots up from the ground and twists all around the building.

"No. Are you? You don't like heights."

"Which is exactly why I want to do this with you."

Tag eyes me with a wary look. "Is everything okay?"

"Why wouldn't it be?"

"You don't take risks, Liv."

"So? Life doesn't always have to be neat and orderly."

"No, but it's a random weeknight, so seems strange to be going down this souped-up slide."

I throw a thumb behind my shoulder. "I can do it on my own then."

"No." He stops me before I get two steps away. "I never said that. Just checking in to make sure that everything is okay."

"I'm good."

He doesn't believe me, but drops it as we head towards the ticket booth.

"Two riders, please."

"Fill out the waiver. Thirty-six pounds."

I tap my card to the reader and grab two clipboards.

"A waiver? This is definitely not what I thought we'd be doing tonight," Tag mutters under his breath.

"I really can do this by myself."

"And let you have all the fun? No way." He smiles at me as he scrawls his name on the bottom line.

"Did you read any of this?"

"Don't sue if you die. Got it."

I roll my eyes at him as I read it over with more due diligence than he used. "I can't believe I'm with someone that doesn't read the terms and conditions."

"Baby, does anyone actually read them?"

"I do, yes. And if anything does happen to you, I'll make sure I won't tell you about them."

He smirks at me. "Got it. Now, are we going to make this thing our bitch or what?"

"Let's do it."

Taking the elevator up the small space, the dark walls give way to glass, taking us higher and higher above the city. From here, the lights of London spread out for miles.

My grip on Tag's hand tightens the closer we get to the top. Nerves threaten to take over, but I won't let them.

I want to take this calculated risk. To feel something other than anger and frustration.

A young man sits at the top, looking bored as can be. He doesn't look a day over fifteen.

"You ready?"

He nods to the car-like contraption that sits at the entrance to the enclosed slide that will take us back down to the earth.

"Is he old enough to operate this?" I whisper out of the corner of my mouth.

"Not too late to back out," Tag tells me.

"Not backing out, just confirming the safety of the ride."

"Want me to go first to test it out?" He winks.

"Tag."

He sweeps me into his arms and lays one on me. "If anything happens, feel free to take the elevator back down."

With that, he hops onto the car and he takes off. His happy shouts ring out as he slips away.

Peeking through the window, I can see him whipping through the glass tube as it travels through the metal contraption.

"You going to go or what?" the kid asks.

"Umm, yes."

A new car awaits me as I debate if I really want to do this. I don't want to chicken out. My parents would have frowned upon something like this when I was growing up. It wouldn't be suitable for someone like me to do.

It's that thought that pushes me to do it.

Being perfect hasn't gotten me anywhere with them. So why not take this chance and face my fears?

Tucking my hair into the collar of my sweatshirt, I take my seat and hold on.

"Have fun," he tells me before I'm racing off.

"Ahh!" My shouts echo in the tiny space as the city comes into view. Lights flash before I'm speeding down into darkness.

Shrieks turn to laughter as my fear dissipates. By the time I get down to the bottom, Tag is waiting for me with the happiest look on his face.

"That was amazing." I leap into his arms, peppering his face with kisses. "I can't believe I did it."

"You're a badass, Liv. Don't you ever forget it." He gives me one soul-stirring kiss before pulling back. "Now, let's go grab a drink and something to eat."

This part of the city isn't busy or crowded at this time of night. We find the food stall in the park where the attraction is and I sit at the picnic table while Tag grabs dinner.

Peering up at the slide, it's hard to believe I did that.

"Want to do it again?" Tag asks, sitting down next to me.

I take the canned cocktail from him and crack it open. "Once is good."

"And you had fun?"

I nod. "I always have fun with you. Isn't that the plan?"

I know, I *know*, I need to give him more, but I can't.

Something has me holding back. Holding back the parts of me that I don't like to show the world.

The messy bits that hurt when the people that love me don't show it.

"Fun. Right." A sadness washes over him, but before I can ask him about it, the mask slips back in place. "Well, let's make sure you're fed before we go off doing any more wild and crazy things tonight."

I guess I'm not the only one feeling too many things tonight. Maybe this wasn't the best idea. To fly by the seat of my pants and do something that hurts Tag.

I blow out a breath, wishing I could convey all of this to him. Instead, I rest my head on his shoulder and relish his quiet company.

Until the turmoil of my emotions settles, it's all I can give him right now.

Chapter Twenty-Three

OLIVIA

I'm nervous. I shouldn't be, but I am. After my emotional night with Tag, well, where I dragged him to do something adventurous with me, things have been off.

I don't like the feeling. It's unsettling. And tonight? I don't feel any better because the girls and I are heading to the game.

Mask perfectly in place, I stand outside the rink to await their arrival. Having my girls here will make it easier.

I like Tag. I more than like him, if I'm being honest. But confessing those feelings to him is something I haven't quite figured out how to do.

"You look fab, babe," Imogen calls out as she struts toward me, looking radiant herself. A white, oversized puffer coat is zipped up to her chin with her blonde hair spilling out of a chocolate-brown hat.

"Thanks." I tug at the bottom of my thick wool peacoat. It's a plain black and matches my own black hat. I left my hair down for tonight and decided to curl it. I'm not fussy about makeup and only put a light coat of mascara on.

"C'mon. Let's wait for Sienna inside."

Our tickets get scanned as we push through the turn-stile. Groups of people linger on the concourse, buying merch and snacks before the game starts.

"Do you want anything to drink?" Imogen asks, pulling her wallet out of her bum bag.

"Can you grab me a Coke, please?"

She winks at me before queueing. I stand off to the side, keeping an eye on the people entering to find Sienna. As the crowds start to thin, I get anxious as the puck drop draws near.

"Sorry I'm late." Sienna bursts into the arena with a harried look on her face. "The Tube was delayed and I got all out of sorts getting here."

"It's alright," I tell her as she makes her way towards my spot at the same moment Imogen reappears.

"I promise I left on time," she tells me.

"Sure you did." Imogen laughs. "I would like it to be known that I was on time tonight."

"Will we get to meet this man of yours tonight?" Sienna asks, linking her arm with mine and leading us in the direction of our section.

"Maybe."

Finding the seats Tag reserved for us, we're a few rows behind the glass. The players are finishing warm-ups, but my eyes aren't focused on them.

They're focused solely on the man in the suit behind the boards.

Tag.

A man should not look as good as Tag does in a suit. It's dark grey, paired with a light blue shirt and a navy tie.

Damn. I didn't see him today with work and heading home before the game, but he looks good.

Really good.

"How come you've never brought us to games before?" Imogen asks.

"I've asked you if you've wanted to come to games before, but you've never wanted to."

"I think what Imogen means is you've been holding out on us."

"And why is that?" I grab a piece of popcorn from the bucket and pop it into my mouth.

"Because these men are *hot*." Imogen mocks fanning herself as the puck drops.

"Well, you two should know better. I shouldn't have to tell you where the men are."

"Listen to her." Imogen ignores me, turning to Sienna. "She's grown up so much since she started dating Tag."

"I can't with you two some days." I laugh, turning my attention back to the ice.

Before Tag, I doubt I ever would have come to one of the team's games. Work was my life, but I was only interested in the business side of things. Now? Now I'm branching out and doing things I never would have done before.

The players change positions as Tag leans down to talk to one of the players. It's nice to see how crowded the arena is. With the team's record improving, more and more people are flocking to the games. Something I know from spending all my time with Tag.

"Why does the redhead look familiar?" Imogen asks, leaning closer to me.

"You mean Alfie?" I follow her eyes as she checks him out.

"Yeah. Him."

"He was at the bar the night I met Tag."

"That's right." Her eyes widen. "You wouldn't let me talk to him."

"No," Sienna interjects. "She said she could talk to Tag on her own."

"You've definitely been holding out on me." Imogen ignores her. "You'll have to introduce me to him. He's a snack."

I snicker, grabbing my drink and taking a long gulp. I love these two women, but once they get going, they don't stop.

I turn my attention back to the game as Wagner, the center, steals the puck and takes off down the ice.

A thread of tension travels through the crowd as everyone gets to their feet in hopes that he puts the puck in the back of the net.

And that's exactly what he does. The red lamp lights up as fans start cheering.

"Well, that was exciting," Sienna says. "I don't know why I've never been to a hockey game before now."

"You're always welcome to come with me."

Feeling a set of eyes on me, I look around and connect with Tag. He wiggles his fingers at me before play starts.

My heart catches in my chest.

What is he doing to me? I am completely undone at this man. One look from him and I'm a puddle of goo.

"You are so fucking cute. I can't even stand it," Imogen says. "Seriously, that man looks at you like you're better than a Christmas pudding."

"Are you two going to be spending the holidays together?" Sienna asks.

"The holidays?"

I've been so swept up in my own thoughts that I haven't paid much attention to the upcoming holiday.

Crap. We haven't discussed it. It sends a fissure of panic sweeping through me. Why didn't I think to discuss the holidays?

It's not like I can take him home to my parents'. And with such a short break between Christmas and New Year's games, it's not like he really has time to fly home.

"Stop spiraling," Sienna says, resting a hand on my shoulder.

"Well, you asked a question that feels weighted, and I don't know how to answer it."

Grabbing my soda, I take a sip. The cool, effervescent bubbles help to calm my racing thoughts.

It's still too early to be worrying about these things. The team is doing well, but there is still no guarantee Tag will be sticking around after this season. It was a one-year deal. I saw the paperwork. Is he going home at the end of the season? And if he is, does that mean he wouldn't be going home over the holidays?

These are so not the thoughts I wanted to be having tonight. A blinding light is now flashing across my future with Tag.

"You know, you can ask him. It'll solve your problem." Imogen elbows me in the side.

"It won't be too forward?"

"No. You should do it so you don't spend the holiday all on your own."

I spend the rest of the game fretting about it. It's hard to enjoy the win because I'm worrying myself ragged thinking about it.

"C'mon, Livvy. Let's go see the guys. Introduce me to Alfie. That'll take your mind off things."

Not that Imogen needs my help. By the time we make it back to the locker rooms, the guys are already funneling out.

Sienna and Imogen flag down Alfie and Jack as I await the head coach. The minute he spots me, he heads my direction.

"Hey, baby."

"What are you doing for Christmas?" I blurt out before I can get another word out. I groan, dropping my head into Tag's chest. Why can I not be more cool around this man? Not that I've ever been that cool to start with, but still.

"I don't know. Do you have plans for the holidays?" he asks. Cupping the nape of my neck and tilting my head back, he forces me to look him in the eyes.

"No."

Not that I ever have plans, but again, not something I want to tell this man that I've been seeing for the last few months.

"Well, my sister was going to try and come for a visit, but I don't think that's going to happen anymore. And with the games, I can't really go home."

"So that means you're not doing anything?"

I wrap my arms around his waist and pull him closer. Not that he wasn't close before, but I find that when I'm in reaching distance of Tag, I like being able to touch him. He calms me in a way that has never happened before.

"Olivia, do you want to spend the holidays with me?" The corner of his mouth quirks up into a soft smile.

"I would love to spend the holidays with you, Tag."

"Good." He presses a warm kiss to my lips and I sink into his hold. Tag makes me feel all fluttery and ooey gooey inside. I find that I want to feel this more and more.

"Shall we do it at your place or mine?"

"Do you have a Christmas tree?" I ask him. "I have a sad excuse for a tinsel tree that doesn't necessarily need to be seen by others."

"Considering I couldn't get one in my suitcase and I wasn't going to pay to ship it, I actually don't have one."

"Well, maybe that means you and I can go tree shopping beforehand. Maybe spruce up your place a bit."

"I think that sounds perfect, Olivia. Spending my first holidays here with you."

He says it like it's the beginning of a lot more. It has my heart swelling in my chest, burying all the messy feelings that I've been feeling lately.

Because I can't wait to spend this special time with the man who has captured my heart.

From: Stanley Easton III <seaston@londonlight-
ning.co.uk>
Sent: Wednesday, December 17, 2026 7:43 AM
To: Olivia Montrose <omontrose@londonlightning.co.uk>
Subject: Tree

Liv,

Where is the best place to find a tree in London? I
suddenly find myself needing to decorate my flat for the
holidays.

Thanks,
Stanley Easton III
Head Coach - London Lightning

From: Olivia Montrose <omontrose@londonlight-
ning.co.uk>
Sent: Wednesday, December 17, 2026 8:17 AM
To: Stanley Easton III <seaston@londonlightning.co.uk>
Subject: RE: Tree

Mr. Easton,

It might be hard to find a decent tree since Christmas is
next week, but I have a place we can look to.

Why are you in the office so early?

Regards,

Olivia Montrose
Business Department

London Lightning

From: Stanley Easton III <seaston@londonlight-
ning.co.uk>
Sent: Wednesday, December 17, 2026 8:19 AM
To: Olivia Montrose <omontrose@londonlightning.co.uk>
Subject: RE: Tree

Needed to get a jump on studying film for the game on Friday. Belfast has a good team. Besides, someone didn't want to get up, so I figured I'd let her sleep <<side eye emoji>>

I'll need decorations too. I don't want a sad looking tree.

Thanks,
Stanley Easton III
Head Coach - London Lightning

From: Stanley Easton III <seaston@londonlight-
ning.co.uk>
Sent: Wednesday, December 17, 2026 8:36 AM
To: Olivia Montrose <omontrose@londonlightning.co.uk>
Subject: RE: Tree

And not just ornaments. Maybe some garlands too. And a stocking or two.

Thanks,
Stanley Easton III
Head Coach - London Lightning

From: Olivia Montrose <omontrose@londonlight-
ning.co.uk>
Sent: Wednesday, December 17, 2026 8:47 AM
To: Stanley Easton III <seaston@londonlightning.co.uk>
Subject: RE: Tree

This is turning into quite the day it seems.

Olivia Montrose
Business Department
London Lightning

From: Stanley Easton III <seaston@londonlight-
ning.co.uk>
Sent: Wednesday, December 17, 2026 8:48 AM
To: Olivia Montrose <omontrose@londonlightning.co.uk>
Subject: RE: Tree

You really have mastered ignoring some of my comments.

It's my first Christmas here. You don't want it to be a sad
one, do you?

Thanks,
Stanley Easton III
Head Coach - London Lightning

From: Olivia Montrose <omontrose@londonlight-
ning.co.uk>
Sent: Wednesday, December 17, 2026 8:57 AM
To: Stanley Easton III <seaston@londonlightning.co.uk>
Subject: RE: Tree

You make it easy sometimes.

That is the last thing I want. Please confirm availability and I will send an invite to get said Christmas decorations.

Regards,

Olivia Montrose
Business Department
London Lightning

From: Stanley Easton III <seaston@londonlightning.co.uk>
Sent: Wednesday, December 17, 2026 10:05 AM
To: Olivia Montrose <omontrose@londonlightning.co.uk>
Subject: RE: Tree

Confirm availability? Professional Olivia is my favorite. Tomorrow night.

No need for a calendar invite ;)

Thanks,
Stanley Easton III
Head Coach - London Lightning

From: Olivia Montrose <omontrose@londonlightning.co.uk>
To: Stanley Easton III <seaston@londonlightning.co.uk>
New Meeting Request - Holiday Shopping

Thursday, December 18 at 17:00

Location: To Be Determined, followed by a meal

Regards,

Olivia Montrose
Business Department
London Lightning

From: Stanley Easton III <seaston@londonlight-
ning.co.uk>
Sent: Wednesday, December 17, 2026 10:45 AM
To: Olivia Montrose <omontrose@londonlightning.co.uk>
Subject: RE: Tree

You really are my favorite person, Liv. Just so you know.

Thanks,
Stanley Easton III
Head Coach - London Lightning

Chapter Twenty-Four

TAG

"Oh, fuck. Fuck. Just like that, baby."

I fist my fingers in Liv's hair as she sucks my cock deeper into her mouth. Is there a better way to be woken up on Christmas morning than a blow job?

One of her hands plays with my heavy balls as the other works in tandem with her mouth. Those lips of hers are stretched around me, and it takes everything I have not to buck up into her.

She pulls off me and swirls her tongue around the head, lapping up the precum there. A finger trails down the vein on the underside, pushing me that much closer to coming down her throat.

Everything about this woman turns me on. From the lust in her eyes to the way her mouth is sucking me down like it's the best thing she's ever tasted.

"Fuck, I'm close, Liv."

Licking her lips, she swallows me as far as she can. She bobs up and down, squeezing my shaft, and that does it. Liv doesn't let go as she sucks down every last drop of my release.

"Fuck."

Liv sits up onto her heels, her sexy body on display. Even though she was doing all the work, she looks thoroughly fucked—chest flush, nipples tight, and hair a mess. Don't even get me started on her mouth.

"Get down here." I wiggle a finger at her, needing to kiss those luscious lips.

Our kisses are slow and languid as I let my hands roam all over her body. I can't get enough of her. Of her taste. The feel of her weight over me.

I am so completely in love with this woman, it's not even funny.

I pull away and pepper her face with kisses. "Time to return the favor."

She shakes her head, giving me a quick peck before slipping out of bed. "No."

"No? Seriously?"

"Yes. I'm going to go clean up and then make you breakfast while you stay in bed."

I can only ogle her perfect ass while she runs into the bathroom. My body feels as limp as a spaghetti noodle. Needing to clean up myself, I follow behind her.

"You're supposed to be in bed!" she mumbles around her toothbrush.

I give her a light smack on the ass, kissing the crown of her head. "Freshening up then I will follow orders."

She rolls her eyes before spitting and heads back out into the bedroom. The sounds of Liv banging around in the kitchen have a smile etched onto my face. This is one of the things I missed when living on my own. Another person being in my space.

When I came to London, I had no intentions of finding another person. Having been divorced, I was good on my own.

It was all a lie I was telling myself.

I guess I just needed to find the right woman. Which, I apparently had to go to a different continent to find. It's made spending the first holiday away from home that much easier. I don't know why she's not spending it with her family, but I'm sure it has something to do with her parents.

Following Liv's orders, I slip into a pair of boxers and crawl back into bed as she walks back into the room, carrying a tray. She's wearing her wool socks—because her feet are always cold—and my sweatshirt that falls to just above her knees. I don't think I've ever seen a sexier sight.

"What'd you make?" I stretch, sitting up and resting my back against the wall.

"Bacon butties." Liv sets the tray on the nightstand before I pull her back onto the bed with me. Her lips taste of her peppermint toothpaste.

"You really are trying to turn me British, aren't you?"

She cups my cheeks, staring up at me. "You have not lived until you've tried a bacon butty. And trust me, Tag, I make the best ones."

"Oh, you do, do you?"

She nods. "Yes. Now time to eat."

Grabbing the tray, I set it on my lap so we can each grab a butty. My stomach rumbles at the smell of bacon. A brown sauce drips from the side of the crusty bread. Taking a hearty bite, the flavors explode on my tongue.

The bacon is crispy, the roll soft, and the sauce has a touch of a kick to it. Damn, this thing is good.

I take three more bites, barely breathing between each.

Liv has a smug look on her face. "Told you."

I roll my eyes at her. "Yes, yes, you did."

Liv takes a demure bite, licking a bit of sauce off her

finger. Fuck if that image of her doesn't make me want to stay in bed all day. "I can make you another if you'd like."

I shake my head. "You'll have to teach me."

"What if it's my secret recipe?"

"Is it your secret recipe?" I quirk a brow at her as I gobble down the rest of the sandwich.

"No." She laughs. "It's a standard recipe, but I like to add a little something to the sauce."

"What's that?"

"Worcestershire sauce. I like the bite it gives the sandwich."

"Delicious." I wipe my mouth with the napkin she brought and hop out of bed. "Now it's time to give you your Christmas gift."

"Wait, you got me a Christmas gift? We said we weren't doing gifts."

Grabbing a sweatshirt from my closet, I yank it over my head and go to the small tree that sits on the coffee table.

"And I ignored you."

"Tag!" Liv shrieks from the bedroom. "All I did was make you breakfast."

Strolling back into the room, I hold the poorly wrapped box behind my back. Wrapping presents is a skill I've never been able to master.

"You gave me a bacon butty and a blow job. How could I ever want anything more than that?"

"Stanley Easton. You cannot give me a present for that in exchange."

I love that she can't even say the word. My sweet, posh Olivia. Fuck, do I ever love her. Which is why I got her a present. I'm head over heels for this woman, and I wanted to get her something to express this. Telling her? Well, I don't know if she's at the same point as me, so I don't want to scare her away.

Baby steps.

"Open it."

Liv pops open the box and her jaw drops. "Tag. This is beautiful."

It's a simple gold necklace with three small diamonds set in the middle of the chain. Nothing fancy or over-the-top.

"Not as beautiful as you." I take the necklace from the box and clasp it around her neck.

Olivia cups my cheeks. "You are so cheesy, but I love it."

Her eyes are sparkling as she drops her forehead to mine. The faint smell of her perfume makes me want to blurt out how much I love her. How much she means to me.

Before I can get the words out, a knock echoes in the tiny apartment.

"Who's that?" Olivia asks.

"I have no idea."

But needing to be somewhat put together to find out, I grab the sweats rumpled on the floor and step into them.

Pulling open the door, I'm met with a surprise.

"Natalie. What the hell are you doing here?"

"Is that any way to greet your favorite sister?"

I roll my eyes at her and open the door for her. I don't let her get far before hugging her to me. I didn't realize just how much I missed her until now.

"Umm, who's this?" Liv pops out of the bedroom, dressed for the day.

Damn, that's a shame.

"Liv, this is my sister, Natalie. Natalie, this is…" My girlfriend? Shit. We never actually discussed this, and I don't want to say the wrong thing. Especially on Christmas.

"Olivia." Liv walks over to us. "His girlfriend."

Well, I guess that clears it up.

"Girlfriend? Wow. You didn't tell me you were seeing anyone." Natalie elbows me in the stomach. "I hope he treats you better than he treats me."

I roll my eyes at my sister's dramatics. She is the spitting image of me with the same brown hair and dark eyes. Right down to the smile that is on her face.

"And how exactly do I treat you?" I ask, grabbing her suitcase and dragging it inside.

"Leaving me all alone on the holidays?" she teases me. "What a great brother."

"Yes, leaving you with your husband was such a hardship."

Natalie waves me off and drops down onto the sofa with a sigh. "If only he could've come with me."

"Everything okay?" I ask, heading into the kitchen to start another pot of coffee. Liv takes a seat on the chair next to the sofa.

Natalie smiles at me as the beans start to brew. "Oh, we're great. We couldn't get two last-minute tickets, so we celebrated yesterday morning and he was going to spend today with his parents. I made the incorrect assumption you would be alone."

"Sorry, I guess that's my fault," Liv says, looking nervous.

Sitting up, Natalie spins to look at her. "Don't be sorry. I'm happy he's not spending the holidays alone."

"Have you ever been to London?" Liv asks.

Natalie shakes her head. "No, this is my first time."

"Well, Tag has practice tomorrow, so why don't I show you around? Maybe we can get tea."

Natalie's face lights up at the offer. "I would love that. Considering he has told me nothing about you."

"That is definitely his fault." Liv laughs.

"Okay, I don't need you two ganging up on me hour one."

Natalie winks at Liv. "No, we'll save that for tomorrow."

The two of them are chatting away, and damn, if this isn't the perfect day. Getting to spend the holiday with my sister and Liv?

I don't think anything could be more perfect.

Chapter Twenty-Five

OLIVIA

"Seeing as you've never been to London, is there anything in particular you'd like to see?" I ask Natalie.

With Tag off at practise, I didn't want Natalie to be alone today. Try as I might, I'm nervous. It feels important for her to like me.

"Everything?" She laughs as the Tube rattles on towards central London. "That probably doesn't help much."

I smile back at her. "I'll make sure you see everything then."

"Do you have a favorite place?"

"The Tower Bridge. It's wonderful. I love the views of the city, especially at night."

Thinking about that evening with Tag, just the two of us on the walkway, has a flush creeping up my cheeks. It is very much something I don't want to be thinking about while out with Tag's sister.

"Maybe Tag can take me when he gets back."

"How long are you here for?" The tinny voice echoes

over the speakers as we pull into the station. Peeking at the sign, I stand. "This is our stop."

She follows me out in the crush of people. Even with the holidays upon us, it's still crowded.

"Until the twenty-ninth. I want to be home for New Year's with the family."

"It's too bad they couldn't join you."

"I'm hoping this will be the first of many trips." Natalie waves me off. "Between you and me, how is Tag doing here? With the team and all?"

"He's fine."

Natalie links her arm with mine as I lead us toward the stately palace. Its presence looms large in the city.

"That's what he said. I want the real answer."

Peering one eye up at her, I take her in. It's easy to see that the two of them are related. They have the same easy-going personality that I never had.

"The team is doing well, and from what I can tell, he likes London."

Natalie stops at the crosswalk as cars zip by us. "He likes *you*."

"I…"

I turn into a bumbling idiot. I shouldn't. I know Tag likes me. It's a feeling that is reciprocated.

Being with Tag is unlike anyone I've ever been with. He makes me feel big, scary feelings. Ones that I'm not quite used to having. It's a battle to not let them overwhelm me, but to let myself feel them when I'm with him.

Because Tag makes me feel safe, like I can explore everything with him.

"I honestly didn't know if he'd ever find someone to make him happy again after his divorce."

"Really?" The light changes and the white sign to cross blinks. I lead her across the busy road, packed with people taking in the historical sites. "Tag told me he got divorced, but only that his wife left him because he stopped playing."

"She was a piece of work. None of us liked her, but Tag loved her, so we tolerated her. She never treated him like he should have been. To be honest, I thought Tag was running away from his problems by coming here."

"If it makes you feel better, I don't think that's true."

"I would have to agree, now that I've seen the two of you together."

A comfortable silence falls between the two of us as Natalie snaps photo after photo of the iconic structure in front of us. Tourists are trying to get the King's guards to crack, to no avail.

"Here. Let's take one and send it to Tag."

Natalie opens her camera and flips it around onto us. Her smile is bright as I lean in, but she tugs me the rest of the way so our cheeks are touching.

She holds the phone up so we can see it, and it's cute. My cheeks are red from the cold. With the walk from the Tube station, it's more time than I like to spend outdoors this time of year. "That's a good one."

"I like it." She taps away on her phone before the whoosh sound echoes.

"Why don't we grab a spot of tea?" I ask her. "Are you hungry at all? I know the best spot around the corner."

Her eyes light up. "That sounds delightful. Lead the way."

The cold London day has started to seep into my bones. Following the sidewalk around the palace, the entrance to the café is just ahead of us. People bustle by as I open the door for Natalie. A wall of warmth greets us.

It's not crowded, which is why it's one of my favorite spots in London. It might not be the closest to where I live, but it's cosy. Old floral wallpaper is peeling at the corners.

A few wood-top tables are spread out, with mismatched throw pillows that sit on the bench. Teapots hang from a rack in the front of the shop.

The aroma of tea is thick in the air.

"Why don't you grab a table and I'll order?"

"Sounds great."

"Any kind of tea you want?"

"Surprise me."

Taking off my gloves, I stuff them in my pockets as I order our tea and sandwiches.

A white, ceramic teapot covered in painted roses, filled with hot water and tea leaves to steep, is set on the tray, complete with two strainers for the tea leaves and matching pink cups.

"We'll bring the rest out to you shortly."

"Thank you."

I pay for everything and grab the tray and walk over to our table.

"English breakfast, or as we like to call it, black tea. You can't come to England without having it," I tell her, taking the seat across from her.

"It smells delicious."

"It's my favorite." I arrange the teacups and strainers while the tea steeps. The earthy aroma warms me from the inside out. "I usually take mine with a spot of milk, but you can also do sugar."

"Milk sounds good," Natalie tells me.

I nod, taking the pot and pouring the steamy liquid into each cup. The liquid runs dark. Perfect.

I add a splash of milk to each and hand hers over.

"Cheers." Natalie clinks her pink teacup against mine.

"Cheers." I take a small sip, letting the flavors linger on my tongue. Holding the ceramic cup, I let the warmth sink into my cold fingers.

"How long have you been working for the team?" Natalie asks, setting her drink down on the saucer.

"Since I graduated in the spring."

"Big hockey fan?"

I laugh, shaking my head. "Honestly? Not before. It was the first offer that I got in uni, so I took it. I thought it would be a lot harder to find a job, but I'm finding I actually like hockey now."

Her eyes are searching as she sips her tea. "A particular coach wouldn't have anything to do with that, now would he?"

"Stop it."

I drink my tea so I have something to do with my hands. I don't know why talking about Tag always gets me so flustered. It's not like I've never had a boyfriend before. But maybe it's because Tag is the first person that could mean something. Sure, the team is doing well, and it's likely the team will renew his contract, but it's hard to think about the future when Tag's is so uncertain.

A three-tier stand arrives at the table—savory, finger sandwiches on the bottom, scones with clotted cream in the middle, and sweets on top.

"This looks amazing." Natalie is quick to take her sandwiches and set them on her plate. "I'm so glad you brought me here."

"I like that you can pop in and get tea without having to wait or book a table."

"For these sandwiches? I'm surprised it's not busier." Her face is full of delight.

Conversation with Natalie is easy. She tells me about her family back home—something I don't really tell her about—while she asks more questions about work and Tag.

No surprise there.

"I don't know if I could live here," Natalie says, biting into her perfectly baked scone. "I would eat this every day if I could."

"Isn't it delicious?"

I grab my scone and slather clotted cream and jelly on it. I never let myself indulge like this. I have my afternoon cup with a digestive, but scones? Sweets? Sandwiches?

It's a rarity I get all of this.

"I'm really glad we got to spend time together. I can see why my brother likes you," Natalie tells me as we finish our drinks and shrug back into our coats.

"Really?"

"Don't sound surprised. He's not the only one in the family that likes you."

I don't miss the weight of her words. Saying she likes me is more than I could have hoped for, even more so since they never liked Tag's ex-wife. Butterflies swarm in my belly.

"I like you too," I tell Natalie as we head outside. "I'm glad I got to know you better."

"Me too."

As far as unplanned days off work go, this was a good day. Natalie is an easy person to be around, just like her brother.

The one person I want to be around all the time.

Falling for a man like Tag is messing up every idea I had for my life. Maybe it's time I change my plan…

Chapter Twenty-Six

OLIVIA

"You know I don't need a fancy restaurant, right?"

I burrow closer into Tag's side as the cold air nips at my skin.

"When you said you wanted to dress up for the holiday, I figured it required somewhere nicer. But it's still to your liking, babe."

"I guess I'll allow it."

The team will be traveling over New Year's Eve, so Tag and I decided to celebrate early. Which meant it was the perfect time to wear the new dress I got with the girls.

Something I didn't let Tag see when he picked me up.

That will be for later.

"I wish we didn't have an away game," Tag tells me as he opens the door into the restaurant. People linger in the small lobby of the Italian bistro.

"If only I could go with you."

"Why can't you?"

The party in front of us heads to their table as we move forward. "Well, I…"

I try to think of a reason, but I can't. In the past, I've

always spent New Year's Day planning the new year. There's something about starting off the year on the right foot that makes me feel settled.

Not that I feel the need to divulge that little secret to Tag.

"Easton." Tag gives the hostess his name.

"Right this way."

A hand at the small of my back guides me through the restaurant. Gold sconces flicker as noise hums through the space. White fabric drapes from the walls as we're led to a table with red leather seats.

"Thank you." I smile at the hostess as I slip out of my peacoat.

"You've been hiding this all night?"

An appreciate gaze wanders down my body, heat trailing in its wake. The square, black neck is simple, the dress clinging to my curves and hitting just above my knees.

Simple, but classy.

Pressing up onto the toes of my heels, I drop a peck onto Tag's cheek. "You like?"

"If I saw this before we left, I would not have taken you out tonight."

"Well then." I drop into the chair Tag pulls out. "I guess that means you'll be coming home with me tonight."

He drops his lips to my ear. "As if you could keep me away."

Watching as he takes the seat opposite me, he is striking. Hair is windswept. The white button-up is rolled up to the elbows, and the veins of his forearms flex as he leans across the table.

Tag is so effortlessly sexy, it's hard to take my eyes off him.

Our waitress comes over to take our drink order before leaving.

"Back to this whole coming with me on my trip…" Tag trails off, holding his hand out on the table. Grasping it and basking in the warmth, it's hard to remember the reasons *not* to go with him.

"I could be convinced."

"Really?" A smile slides across his face. "How can I convince you?"

"Well," I drag a finger over the lines in his palm, "are you allowed to sneak out after the game?"

Tag beams at me. "I'm the coach. I think I can manage that."

"Well then, maybe I might join you."

I waggle my eyebrows at him before taking the menu and perusing it.

"Might? That's it?"

I peer over at him. "There's a high likelihood that it will be a yes."

"Good. I don't want to ring in the new year without you."

I hide my smile in the menu. Ever since Christmas, things have been good with Tag. Great, even.

I've pushed all thoughts of other less happy things from my mind. Only focusing on Tag? It's been easy.

So easy that I've been considering a change of plans. But that is a thought for another time.

"What sounds good?" I ask.

"You know, that pasta with the chili flakes sounds good."

Heat blooms in my cheeks thinking about that night. That perfect night spent with Tag.

Okay, maybe I'll need to reconsider my plans sooner.

"Mm, that does sound good." I drag the tip of my heel

up his leg. "You know, maybe if I join you, we could have a repeat of that night."

"Fuck, baby. You cannot say things like that in public."

Our drinks are dropped off and our dinner order is placed.

"A taste of your own medicine, isn't it?" I sip on my wine as Tag's eyes darken.

"I guess turnabout is fair play. But you know, we don't have to have a special occasion to reenact that night."

"We really don't."

Conversation switches back to the team and work as dinner comes and we eat our meals. It's the perfect way to spend the evening.

I'm finding this is my favorite way to spend most evenings.

With Tag.

"Have I convinced you to come?" Tag asks after he pays the bill.

"I think you did." Standing, I follow him through the restaurant towards the exit. "Excuse me." I smile at the passing couple as we leave the restaurant. But as Tag holds open the door, my mouth drops. I'm stunned at the couple I see waiting.

"Mum. Dad. What are you doing here?"

Shock doesn't begin to cover it. I can't remember the last time I've seen my parents. They've never bothered to come visit since I moved to the city. When I left for university, their butler is the one that dropped me off.

Moving into my own flat? I did it myself.

"Olivia. I didn't even recognize you." Her gaze drops to my dress. "Have you done something different with your hair?"

If only I'd put my coat on at the table.

"What are you doing here?"

"Eating dinner." Dad adjusts his round, rimless glasses. "Are you well, Olivia?"

"Yes. And you?"

"Adjusting nicely," Mum answers.

Grey threads her hair. In my last year before leaving for London, she was still colouring it. Not anymore, I guess.

I haven't seen them since before graduation. Dad had a work trip and they couldn't make it. Aside from the one text, I don't think I've spoken to them in months.

"Are these your parents?" Tag asks.

"Not now," I hiss. This is not the time to introduce him to my parents.

"Adjusting to what?" I ask, trying to keep my voice calm.

"City life."

"City life? Did you move?"

Dad nods. "I need to be in the city more for work, so we decided to rent a flat here."

"Wow."

They moved to the city and decided not to tell me? A lead weight settles low in my belly.

"Your table is ready," the hostess interrupts.

"Were you going to tell me you live here now?" I ask. "Seems like something you should tell your daughter."

"We're renting, Olivia," Mum says. "It's not permanent."

"Seems pretty permanent if you're having to adjust to life in the city."

"Olivia, we must go. We'd hate to keep the server waiting," Dad says, impatience lacing his voice.

"Umm, okay. Why don't we make plans for dinner?" I ask.

Mum pats my shoulder. "Stand up straight, dear. It is not doing you any favours."

With that parting note, they leave, stealing whatever happiness this evening left me with.

Emotion clogs my throat as I try to make sense of what just happened. A hand at my elbow steers me outside into the cold night.

"Liv?" Tag's voice stirs my thoughts, and the noise of the busy street comes back into focus.

"Hmm?"

"Are you okay?"

"I can't believe they live here and didn't tell me."

It's the only thing I can tell him. I've been trying to call them for months and they couldn't bother texting me? Tell their only child that they are now living in the same city as her?

"Hey." Tag stops me before I can get far. "Talk to me."

I grab my coat from him and slip into it, covering the dress I was excited about earlier. One look from my mother, one scathing comment, and I hate it.

"Can we go home? Not here."

"Okay. I'll get us a cab."

I don't know if I'll be ready to talk to him about this. How do you tell the person you're falling for that the people who are supposed to love you the most don't care?

It's the worst kind of heartbreak.

And my heart is shattered.

From: Stanley Easton III <seaston@londonlight-
ning.co.uk>
Sent: Wednesday, January 7, 2026 9:07 AM
To: Olivia Montrose <omontrose@londonlightning.co.uk>
Subject: Meeting

Liv,

I have a few questions regarding the paperwork I filled out
at the beginning of the season about my lease. Can you
meet with me to review it?

Thanks,
Stanley Easton III
Head Coach - London Lightning

From: Olivia Montrose <omontrose@londonlight-
ning.co.uk>
Sent: Wednesday, January 7, 2026 11:03 AM
To: Stanley Easton III <seaston@londonlightning.co.uk>
Subject: RE: Meeting

Mr. Easton,

At the current time, I am working on another project and
will not be able to review this with you. Please email Joe
Banks to address this matter.

Regards,

Olivia Montrose
Business Department
London Lightning

From: Stanley Easton III <seaston@londonlightning.co.uk>
Sent: Wednesday, January 7, 2026 11:17 AM
To: Olivia Montrose <omontrose@londonlightning.co.uk>
Subject: RE: Meeting

Why can't you help me? I don't want to work with this other person.

Thanks,
Stanley Easton III
Head Coach - London Lightning

From: Stanley Easton III <seaston@londonlightning.co.uk>
Sent: Wednesday, January 7, 2026 2:02 PM
To: Olivia Montrose <omontrose@londonlightning.co.uk>
Subject: RE: Meeting

Are you going to ignore me? I know where you work. I can just come over there to talk to you. Seriously, what's going on?

Thanks,
Stanley Easton III
Head Coach - London Lightning

From: Joe Banks <jbanks@londonlightning.co.uk>
Sent: Wednesday, January 7, 2026 2:18 PM
To: Stanley Easton III <seaston@londonlightning.co.uk>
Subject: Lease Paperwork

Mr. Easton,

Miss Montrose informed me you had some questions regarding your lease paperwork that you completed on arrival. Seeing as how she is busy with other projects at the present time, please direct any concerns to me and I will promptly address them.

Thank you,
Joe Banks
Business Department Manager
London Lighting

Chapter Twenty-Seven

TAG

"You want to grab lunch after film?" Alfie asks. "I want to go over a few more things about the upcoming game with Manchester."

Manchester is leading the league. They've been on fire this season. Their center is unstoppable.

"Can we meet later this afternoon? I've got plans."

"With Liv?" He smirks.

"Yes."

I don't actually have plans with her, but I'm hoping she might be up for lunch. Ever since we bumped into her parents, I've seen her sparingly.

She didn't come with me over New Year's, and in the few days since then, it's been almost radio silence.

"Things seem to be going well."

"More or less." I shrug a shoulder. "Now, let's go because it's time to study film."

"You got it."

The team is already gathered in the locker room when I pull up the footage from Manchester's last game.

We work through our plan of attack, highlighting their best players and their go-to moves.

"Kadlec tends to favor the left side of the ice. He pulls the defensemen over there, leaving Singleton all on his own. It gives them great opportunities from that side of the ice. Don't let them trick you into leaving him open. Play your position to give Simmons the best chance in the net."

"He tends to shoot stick side, Coach," Simmons says. "I'll watch for the fake out, but I'm ready."

"I know you are," I confirm.

Manchester might be the best team in the league, but we have the most heart. I see it day in and day out with these guys.

Sure, we've had our fair share of losses this season, but they keep moving forward. They study film, see what they need to improve upon, and do it. It makes my job as their coach that much easier.

I love these guys and hope to keep coaching them for years to come.

"Alright. Let's hit the weight room before taking the ice. I want to run some conditioning drills. Make sure we keep up with them on the ice."

"Yes, Coach," they echo. I watch as they funnel out toward the weight room.

"I'll be back before we hit the ice," I tell Jack and Alfie.

"Tell Liv we said hi," Alfie says.

I wave at him before heading to my office to grab the sandwiches I picked up earlier. Hopefully getting Liv's favorite will warm her up.

I wave to the people in her department as I pass through.

"Hey, Liv." I knock on the door and peek my head inside. "Lunch?"

She peeks one eye open at me before going back to her computer screen. "Not today."

"Everyone has to eat." I smile at her, walking inside and closing the door behind me.

"Not today. I have a meeting in twenty minutes to discuss the new league initiatives and how they will affect the bottom line of the team."

"That's still twenty minutes. I got your favorite sandwich."

Liv smooths a nonexistent piece of hair back into place. It's perfectly smoothed into a low bun at the nape of her neck. Her blouse is buttoned up to her neck and her blazer is pressed.

"That's twenty minutes I have to prepare. I will eat after."

I blow out a breath and rest my elbows on my knees. "Liv, talk to me. What's going on?"

"Nothing is going on. I'm busy. I have a lot of projects going on after the holidays and I don't have time for things I used to."

"You mean me?"

It shouldn't sting as much as it does.

My schedule is crazy. Between practice, games, and travel, I devote every spare minute of time to Liv. It's not a sacrifice because I love her. But trying to get twenty minutes from her is too much to ask?

"Tag." Liv finally turns her attention to me, a sad look on her face. "You're asking too much of me."

"To see you? Sorry I'm such a burden," I scoff.

"You're not a burden!" she shouts. Her eyes go wide before she takes a deep breath, running a hand down her blouse. "But you're not the plan."

I hate that fucking word of hers. *Plan.*

Everything in Olivia's life has to be perfect. Lined up.

Neat as a pin. I knew that the minute I ran into her at the rink on my first day.

Ever since then, she's been showing more and more of herself to me. I get to see the messy side of her. The one that she doesn't show just anyone.

Now it's back to the prim and proper side of her. Ever since her parents showed up, she was thrown for a loop. She won't let me in. Won't talk to me about anything.

"So? Screw your plan."

"Tag. I can't do this anymore."

"What?"

Those are the last words I expected to hear come out of her mouth.

Can't do this anymore?

"What happened, Liv? We had a really good thing going here, and then one run-in with your parents and you're different."

"That's the real me. *Is* the real me."

"No, it's not. The real you is the one that takes risks. Does things that she normally wouldn't. Lets her hair down and has fun."

Liv shakes her head. "No. That's the messy Liv. The real me is the one that has a plan. If I want everything by the time I'm twenty-eight, I need to get serious about my life."

"And the fact that I love you means nothing?"

Not exactly the way I wanted to confess my feelings to her, but I guess this is what we're doing today.

"No. This is my life, Stanley, and I get to say what I want it to be."

"That's it? There's no chance of a future because I make life messy?"

"That's it."

I drop the sandwiches on her desk and stand, but not before I leave her with parting words.

"Olivia, if you learn one thing from me, let it be this. Life isn't perfect. It's messy and raw and real, and that's what you have to look forward to, plan or not. I don't know what number your parents did on you, but we all deserve to have someone in our lives that loves us. And make no mistake, Liv. I love you. I love every side you give me. Even the ones you think might not be perfect. You're perfectly imperfect, and it's what I love most about you."

I drink my fill of the woman sitting at her desk. The one that isn't showing me an ounce of emotion. Her mask is in place—the one that doesn't show the world anything —and I know I've lost her.

"Take care, Stanley."

I guess I really didn't know Liv as well as I thought I did.

I don't say anything else as I leave her office. There's nothing else to say. Because what else is there when the woman you love breaks your heart?

Chapter Twenty-Eight

OLIVIA

IMOGEN

Think you can peel yourself away from Tag long enough to have dinner with us tonight?

SIENNA

We miss you!

OLIVIA

I saw you two last weekend

IMOGEN

That was last weekend

IMOGEN

I'm beginning to forget what you look like

You're being dramatic

SIENNA

Question still stands

SIENNA

Are you free tonight?

Yes

> I can cook dinner if you want

IMOGEN

There's that new Japanese restaurant
opening I want to go to

IMOGEN

Is that okay?

> Sure

IMOGEN

Great

IMOGEN

I'll make a reservation

> 7?

IMOGEN

Yes

SIENNA

See you then xx

IMOGEN

Tell Tag we said hiiii x

I lock my phone and stuff it into my desk drawer, ignoring the pain that slices through my heart at the mention of Tag.

I haven't been able to bring myself to tell these two about me and Tag. It's not like *not* telling them is going to make it any less real.

But it's better this way.

Since Tag and I ended things, life has been quiet. Orderly.

I know what every minute of each day will bring.

Exactly what I need.

Shuffling a stack of papers around on my desk, I try to get my head back into the reports I'm working on. The numbers are blending together.

I can't focus. Why can't I focus? Things are supposed to be easier now that my life is back on track. My five-year plan is exactly what I want.

Then why do I feel so terrible?

Resigning myself to not getting any work done today, I send an email to my boss letting him know I'm taking the rest of the afternoon off and head home.

Another thing that is unlike me.

Since I started work, I have never taken a day off, other than the one I spent with Natalie. Even when I was feeling under the weather, I would answer emails from home.

I never wanted people to think they couldn't rely on me.

I blow out a breath as I slip into my coat and wrap my scarf around my neck. A cold, biting wind has its fingers in the weather, and I hate it.

I bow my head as I walk straight into it.

My cheeks are frozen by the time I make it back to my flat. Sinking onto the sofa, everything feels empty.

Dull.

The pillows are exactly where they should be. The bookshelf is clean. The bed? Made with military precision before I left for work.

Everything is exactly as I like it. Maybe if I take a short nap before dinner tonight, I'll feel better.

Kicking off my heels and throwing my coat over the back of the sofa, I head into my room to lie down.

But it does nothing.

My mind is a whirling mess of thoughts.

I've tried calling my parents since bumping into them at the restaurant, but no surprise, my calls have gone unanswered.

I did everything right growing up.

Got a perfect score on every test.

Played the piano to perfection.

Was the perfect daughter anytime guests came to the house.

And yet, something about me isn't good enough.

I lie for hours staring at the ceiling. Tears come and go as I try to stave off everything I'm feeling. Maybe dinner with Imogen and Sienna will help me see things in a better light.

Seeing that it's nearing seven, I realise I'm going to be late. For the first time in my life.

Grabbing the first pair of shoes I find, I hurry out of my flat and hail a taxi. I fire off the address of the new restaurant and watch as the city flies by.

When the cab stops in front of the restaurant, I tap my card to the reader and hop out. There's a line around the block, but I know Imogen was able to secure a reservation.

My friends give me funny looks as I'm shown to our table.

"What's wrong?" The moment I sit down, Imogen and Sienna are on me.

"Why is something wrong?"

Imogen makes a dramatic show of checking her watch. "It is ten minutes after seven. You're late."

"Only a few minutes." I grab my napkin and rest it on my lap.

Sienna looks at me like I have three heads. "You're never late. On time is late for you. Actually being late? I don't think it has ever happened."

"Can we order drinks?" I ignore them, picking up the menu and giving it a quick scan, not really seeing anything.

"Oh, no." Imogen takes the menu from me. "We are not ordering drinks until you tell us what is going on."

"Nothing is going on." I don't sound convincing, even to myself.

"Liv, darling. Your hair is down. You are wearing black pants with navy shoes. Seriously, something is wrong with you, and now I'm worried." Imogen scoots her chair closer to me. "What's wrong? Did something happen with Tag?"

I burst into tears. No subtle tear sliding down my cheek. Deep, heaving sobs in the middle of the restaurant.

"Oh, Olivia." I can't hear whose voice tries to comfort me over the sound of my own cries.

"What happened, darling?"

I can't get any words out as I struggle to take in any form of breath.

"We…we…"

"Deep breaths," Sienna coos, stroking my hair. "Take a deep breath."

I try, but it hurts. My body aches with the pain of losing the man I love.

"It's okay, Liv. It's okay." Imogen rubs my back as the two of them try to calm me down.

I don't know how long the two of them comfort me, but it helps. The tears don't stop, but my breathing evens out.

"We weren't a match," I confess.

"I don't believe that for a second," Imogen says. "We saw the two of you together. You were perfect together."

"It's true," Sienna agrees. "That man loves you."

I shake my head. "No. He loved the idea of me. He made things messy. I need my plan."

"Liv, I think you need a little tough love," Imogen says. "I love you, darling. You're one of my closest friends—"

"But?" I interrupt.

"But your plan is crap. It was designed to make your parents love you, when they were the worst humans. You are one of the best people we know. You will do anything for your friends and you love us fiercely."

"I agree," Sienna says. "Tag was the perfect man for you because he brought you out of your shell. He made you see that you deserve love. That you are worthy of it."

The tears start flowing again. Our waiter spots us and, seeing the state I'm in, turns to leave.

"My parents really did a number on me, didn't they?" I try to laugh it off, but I can't.

"You know," Imogen says, "you could benefit from talking to someone about this."

"I'm talking to you two, aren't I?"

Sienna passes a tissue from her purse. "I think she means a therapist. A professional."

"Really?"

They both nod. Sienna brushes a stray lock of hair out of my face. "We love you, but this situation? I think you really should talk to someone. Because neither of us want to see you lose Tag."

"It feels like I'm admitting defeat."

"No, love. It means you realise you need help and are being an adult by seeking it out."

"Yes," Sienna agrees. "I think it'll help you more than you know."

"But Tag…"

"Focus on you, love. That's the most important thing to start with. Tag will come later because I believe he was always your plan."

Maybe Tag was the plan. But until then, I think they're right.

Working on myself and then figuring out what to do next.

I only hope I didn't ruin the best thing I ever had in my life.

Chapter Twenty-Nine

OLIVIA

SIENNA

Good luck today, love

IMOGEN

Remember, as someone who has been to a lot of therapists, tell them how you're feeling

IMOGEN

It will suck, but we're here for you

SIENNA

Yes. Come over after and we can decompress with you

OLIVIA

I love you guys

IMOGEN

We love you

SIENNA

xx

L ocking my phone, I stuff it into my bag and fold my hands into my lap. I've never been more nervous in my life. Plain, beige walls hold photos of trees and the beach. My guess is it's to put people at ease, but it's not helping. Can anything really help when you're going to spill your guts out to a stranger?

I know it helped Tag after his divorce, but will it help me? And the thought of Tag again makes my heart feel like it's crumbling out of my chest.

"Miss Montrose?" a warm voice calls out for me. Not that it matters because I'm the only one in here. It belongs to an older woman with short, curly brown hair. Glasses sit perched on her nose. "I'm Hannah."

"Hi." The plastic chair creaks as I stand, grabbing my coat and bag to follow her back to another room.

This one feels less sterile. Soft music is playing, and the sweet scent of lavender perfumes the air. Plush pillows sit on the couch, and a crystal glows on the small table. There are no pictures of trees or the beach, but bright swatches of color. I don't know why, but these feel more calm. Soothing.

"You can take a seat on the couch," Hannah tells me, taking the seat opposite me. "Make yourself comfortable."

"Thank you."

Sitting down, I set my bag and coat next to me and cross one leg over the other.

"First time seeing a therapist?" she asks.

I nod. "Is it that obvious?"

"It's okay. We all have things we need to address at different times. Why don't you tell me what brought you in today?"

"Okay."

Perspiration dots my brow as heat chokes my throat.

"Take your time, Olivia." She gives me a warm smile.

"It's hard for me to talk about these things."

"This is a safe space. Tell me when you're ready."

"It's just…my parents didn't like emotions. They were too messy. It was easier to keep things inside."

"Do you still feel like emotions are messy?" she asks.

"Yes?" I clear my throat. "Things had to be perfect growing up. The better grades I got, the more attention I got from my parents. If I got a bad grade, I got a stern look and that was it. There was no room for messy things like feelings."

"Emotions are messy. You're allowed to feel messy."

"That's something I've heard before."

"But you don't believe it?"

"It's hard when I grew up *not* believing it. At least not until…"

It's the first time I'm talking with this woman and I don't know how much I want to divulge.

"Until what?"

Well, I guess she took care of that.

"I met someone. Someone I really liked."

"And how is that going?"

"It's not. I ended things."

She gives me an understanding nod. "Why did you end things?"

"It got too messy. He wasn't in my plan."

"Messy because you were feeling things?"

I can only nod my head because thinking of Tag is too painful. My chin quivers.

"What if I told you messy things can be wonderful?"

That grabs my attention. "How?"

"It seems this person you met meant something to you? Probably still does?"

I nod and she continues.

"Maybe this person was showing you how life could be.

It doesn't have to be perfect and planned out, but can be messy and imperfect together."

"But…I had a plan."

"Okay. Tell me about your plan."

Shifting, I pull my legs under my butt and sink back into the couch. I pick at a stray thread in the hem of my jumper.

"I wanted to find a nice guy, get married, have kids, get a dog, and find a good flat in the city."

Hannah recrosses her legs and adjusts her glasses. "It seems to me you're already following your plan."

"But Tag isn't the right guy."

"Says who?"

"My parents wouldn't approve."

"Ah."

"Oh my God." The air leaves my lungs. "The plan I've always had in mind came from my parents."

With not much family, it was the three of us. It was their marriage that was the model for what I wanted in life. Dad went to work, Mum stayed home and then had dinner and a drink ready. I would do my schoolwork, eat with them, then go back to my room.

"I created an entire life plan based off people that never showed me love." Tears well in my eyes before spilling over.

Hannah nods. "It's hard when the people that are supposed to love us don't show us that. If we don't have a model of a healthy relationship, it can be hard to find one as an adult. You have still tried to be the person they would approve of even now."

I go on to explain to her about my parents moving to the city and our run-in at the restaurant.

"After what happened, it's clear they don't care." I

brush an angry tear away. "And I pushed away the one person who actually did."

Hannah holds out the box of tissues to me, and I grab one. Now that the tears have started, it's hard to keep them inside.

"I feel so stupid," I confess.

"You're not," Hannah corrects me. "Keeping a lot of these emotions repressed and bringing them to the forefront of your focus is hard. We don't know what we don't know."

I sniffle. "I'm feeling very messy right now."

"It's okay, Olivia. Messy is okay."

I dab the tears on my cheek, letting the soft music flow into me as I take deep breaths.

"Tell me how you're feeling," Hannah says.

"I'm confused. I'm sad, but at the same time, it feels good to realize this."

"It's hard. But I'm going to give you some homework."

I smile at her. "I didn't realize I'd have work to do for this."

"Sometimes. I think you'd benefit from journaling your feelings. Whether it's sad or happy, I want you to sit with them. Feel them. It's going to be hard, but journaling is a good way to do this."

"Okay. I can do that."

"That's all the time we have for today, but let's make an appointment for next week. You made great progress this week."

"Thank you, I'd like that."

After making another appointment, I slip into my coat and walk out. With extra tissues in my pocket. My heart is raw. Everything feels scrubbed down and left open for everyone to see.

Tension builds in my head as I step out into the

sunshine. It feels weird to see the sun shining so bright when I'm a jumbled mess.

I was skeptical when the girls told me I needed therapy to work through my issues. Turns out, they were right. One visit, and I'm learning things about myself.

Maybe it means if I work through them, I could have a future with Tag…

Chapter Thirty

TAG

As if life wasn't shitty enough, the team is playing like crap. We'd been on a hot streak since the holidays but it's come to a grinding halt. Any progress they made was thrown right out the window tonight.

Missed passes. Easy goals let in. High sticking and holding that led to time in the sin bin.

When the final whistle sounds, I can see the collective relief on their faces as they skate off the ice.

And it pisses me off.

"You coming to the locker room?" Jack elbows me in the side. The entire team is gone and the arena is clearing out.

"I'll be there in a minute."

The last thing I need to do is take out my own feelings on the team. Even though they played like crap doesn't mean I have to lash out at them. I've had enough coaches do that to me that I never want to lead a team like that.

We head back to London tomorrow and have one more game this weekend. Maybe we can bounce back and put this game behind us.

The Zamboni comes out to clear the ice, and I take that as my cue to head back toward the locker room.

Heads are hanging and the mood is somber when I step inside.

"It wasn't our best game tonight."

"No kidding," someone mumbles.

That pulls a laugh out of me. "I don't want anyone getting too down about this. So it wasn't our best game? We'll learn from it. We'll study film tomorrow before we play again and learn from this. We've still got a great team and have a shot at making the playoffs."

A few guys mumble in return, but that's all I get.

"Alright. Hit the showers and then I want everyone to turn in early tonight. No going out, straight to bed. You got it?"

"Yes." That gets more of an answer.

By the time we get back to the hotel, the guys at least seem to be in better spirits. Me? I'm ready to crash.

Between the travel and wondering where things went wrong with Liv, I'm exhausted.

"We're getting drinks," Jack tells me matter-of-factly.

"I'm tired." I shake my head.

"Nope." Alfie grabs me by the shoulders and steers me into the hotel bar. "You've been a sad sack and we are not going to let this continue."

"I agree." Jack nods. "We just got our asses handed to us and you're down, so we need a drink tonight."

"Shouldn't the coaches set the example for the team? I told them all to go to bed."

"Coaches' prerogative. We can have a drink. 'Discuss the game.'"

I sigh. "Fine."

Alfie heads to the bar to order a round of pints as Jack and I find a table in the corner for us.

"What's going on? You're usually happier than this."

"Everyone has their off days."

"This is more than an off day," Jack says. "What's wrong?"

Alfie returns with a pitcher and three glasses. He pours us each a glass and passes them around. "Is everything okay with Liv?"

"How much time do you have?"

I gulp down half the lager in one go, wiping my upper lip.

"Shit. Did you two break up?" Alfie asks.

"Yup." Another gulp. At least the beer might help my feelings.

"What happened? You two were so good together," Jack says. "Last I saw, you two were annoyingly happy."

I shrug a shoulder, picking at the coaster that sits on the table. The hotel bar isn't busy, with a few empty tables scattered around the small space. If I can find the words, I'll be able to talk without anyone overhearing.

"Said I didn't fit her plan."

While I, on the other hand, was doing everything to make Liv a part of mine. Isn't that what you do with people you love?

"Fuck, Tag. I'm sorry," Jack commiserates. "There's nothing worse than getting kicked to the curb."

"Tell me about it. I think getting divorced hurt less than this."

I gave Liv every part of me. There wasn't anything I wouldn't do for her. The gulf in my chest widens.

"At least you can focus on hockey," Alfie says. "And we're here for you."

"Whatever you need," Jack reiterates.

"Thanks, guys. I appreciate it." It's nice to have people I can count on here. Ones that I can turn to when things go to shit. I hold up my glass in cheers. "I know we lost, but I'm glad to have you guys by my side out there."

"Cheers, mate."

I take a long drag of beer before pouring myself another glass.

"Now, enough talk about me. Give me the update on your lives."

"You mean besides hockey?" Alfie quirks a brow at me under his glasses. "Pretty much all we do here."

"Then the three of us are all single? Damn, are we sad or what?"

"Hey, I didn't say I was." Jack leans back in his seat and crosses his arms.

"Are you seeing someone? You haven't said anything."

Jack laughs. "Unlike you two, I tend to play things closer to the vest."

"That's a no." Alfie laughs. "I tried to set him up last week and he said that he wasn't interested in dating right now."

"Fucker." Jack flips him off. "It could have been because I was seeing someone."

"Which you're not," Alfie corrects him.

"Fine. I'm not. But I'd like to be."

"You're interested in someone?" I ask.

"Yes, but I'm not telling either of you who."

"I'll tell you I'm interested in someone," Alfie starts, "but you won't like who."

"Why not?" My senses tingle. "Why wouldn't we like this person?"

"It's Imogen."

"Ahh."

One of Liv's best friends.

"Sorry."

I hold up my hands. "No need to be sorry. Is what it is. Feel free to see her."

"If only." He sighs.

"Listen. You two finish the beer. I'll see you in the morning, alright?"

Jack smiles at Alfie. "He lasted longer than we expected."

I flip him off. "Ass."

"Hey. We're here if you need anything," Alfie says.

"Thanks, guys."

Heading back up to my room, I wait on the elevator. Tension gathers in my shoulders. I would have loved to call Liv and talk to her. Hear about her day. Tell her about the game. Get razzed because we lost and won't be the most popular sport in London.

But I don't get any of that.

All I want is Liv, and I get nothing from her now. I hate it.

It's going to be hard to move on when she works for the team. At least we're in separate parts of the building and I don't have to run into her if I don't want to.

At least, that's what I tell myself to make things better.

Because they have to get better, right?

From: Olivia Montrose <omontrose@londonlight-
ning.co.uk>
Sent: Sunday, February 1, 2026 6:07 PM
To: Stanley Easton III <seaston@londonlightning.co.uk>
Subject: Talk soon?

Mr. Easton,

I was hoping you'd have some time to talk soon. I have
some things that I want to discuss if you're open to it.

Regards,

Olivia Montrose
Business Department
London Lightning

From: Olivia Montrose <omontrose@londonlight-
ning.co.uk>
Sent: Wednesday, February 4, 2026 11:17 AM
To: Stanley Easton III <seaston@londonlightning.co.uk>
Subject: RE: Talk soon?

Look, I know it's my fault things ended, but please, can we
talk?

Please…

Olivia Montrose
Business Department
London Lightning

From: Olivia Montrose <omontrose@londonlight-
ning.co.uk>
Sent: Thursday, February 4, 2026 9:58 PM
To: Stanley Easton III <seaston@londonlightning.co.uk>
Subject: RE: Talk soon?

Tag,

Please can we meet?

Liv

Chapter Thirty-One

TAG

"You have any plans tonight?" Alfie asks. "Want to grab a drink once we get back?"

"You don't have to keep me occupied to keep my mind off Liv, you know that, right?" I kick my feet out into the aisle, stretching.

After recovering last weekend with a win, practice went well this week and we managed to scrape out a win tonight.

No matter what these guys do, whenever I slow down enough to let my mind wander, Liv invades my thoughts.

Her leaving wrecked me. I wish I could say it didn't, but it did.

"Next time I'm not going to let you say no."

"Pretty sure you're the reason I'm in this mess."

"It's his fault?" Jack asks from the opposite side of the bus. "What does Alfie have to do with you being a sad sack?"

"He's the one that invited me out my first night here."

The fateful night I met the woman that has since left

me and shattered my heart. But that's not something I need to get into right now.

"Ah. Right." Jack nods. "You sure you don't need that drink?"

I shake my head, resting my hands over my stomach. "Nah. I'm going to head home and crash. I'll be in early before the game tomorrow."

Alfie laughs. "You know you're allowed to enjoy the win, right?"

"Hey. I'm going to enjoy it tonight. Then back to work tomorrow."

The city flashes by as we get closer and closer to our destination. Do I want to spend the night by myself? No. But at least a good night's rest and studying film tomorrow is going to benefit the team.

By the time we're pulling into the parking lot, I'm beat. Guys are filing off the bus as we follow them off.

"I'll see you guys tomorrow, alright?"

"See ya," Alfie calls out.

Grabbing my bag, I stop dead in my tracks. Standing under the security light is Liv.

Olivia.

What the hell?

"Hello."

"What are you doing here?"

"Umm, well…you see," she starts. "You didn't answer my emails."

"That's it?" I heft my bag higher on my shoulder. "I didn't answer your emails?"

Liv adjusts the black hat that sits on her head. "Well, I did ask you to meet. You didn't respond."

"Didn't feel the need to. You said everything you needed to in your office that day."

Liv clears her throat, shifting back and forth on her feet. It's clear she's nervous.

"I, umm, I actually have more to say to you."

"You do?"

I stuff my hands in my pockets so they don't reach out to her on their own accord.

"A lot." Liv pulls out her phone. "I umm, I actually typed it out. If you didn't answer, I was going to email you. I can read that to you if you want."

This is a new side of Liv. I've never seen her nervous. Fidgeting.

"If it's easier for you, go ahead."

Liv clears her throat. "I was wrong, Tag. Growing up, being perfect was the only way to get my parents' attention. Anything less than that and they didn't care. It's in my nature to have everything be neat and orderly. You, Tag, are not neat and definitely not orderly. You made things messy and it scared me. When we ran into my parents, it brought up everything from my childhood. Getting perfect marks in school. Playing the piano. Being the best at everything. But after seeing a therapist, I realized messy is okay. You make me feel messy. And I like that."

"You're seeing a therapist?"

She nods. "It's been hard. Picking at all these feelings from when I was growing up hasn't been easy."

"Then why are you doing it?"

Tears fill her eyes. "Losing you brought it all into stark clarity. I was working towards a plan that lived up to the expectations of my parents. To get their attention. It's taken a lot to realize that I don't need a plan."

I smile. "Who are you and what have you done with my Olivia?"

That earns me a watery smile. "It's been hard, trust

me. It's not easy to acknowledge everything you've wanted in life is to please people that don't love you."

I shake my head, cupping her cheek as the tears escape. "I'll love you, Liv. I'll love you so much that you won't want for anything in life."

Her hands close around my wrists. Fuck. I've missed the feel of her. The softness of her touch that lights me on fire.

"Even if I'm not perfect?"

"I don't want you to be perfect. If that's what you want, fine. But I love all sides of you. The perfect side you show the world. The messy side you only give me. The sad little girl that wants nothing more than to be loved. Let me love you, Olivia. All of you."

"You really want to love me?"

"There's no choice for me, Liv. I love you. From that very first hello, I was a goner for you."

"I love you, Tag. I still have a lot of work to do," Liv confesses. "But I want to be with you. If you'll have me."

I fuse my lips to hers. It's like coming home. It's the best feeling in the world, swallowing her gasps.

I drop my forehead to hers, brushing away her tears. "I've missed you, baby. So fucking much."

"I'm sorry."

I kiss her again—because I can. "I don't want to hear those words again. I'm sorry that you had to go through all of it."

"Thank you for showing me what it's like to be loved, Tag."

"Always. Every day. I will shower you in so much love, Olivia, that you are going to get sick of me."

She shakes her head. "Never. I could never get sick of you, Stanley."

I steal one more kiss. "Then why don't I get started and show you just how much I do love you?"

"Perfect."

From: Olivia Montrose <omontrose@londonlight-
ning.co.uk>
Sent: Thursday, February 26, 2026 10:02 PM
To: Stanley Easton III <seaston@londonlightning.co.uk>
Subject: Tomorrow

Tag,

Care to meet for lunch tomorrow before practice?

From: Stanley Easton III <seaston@londonlight-
ning.co.uk>
Sent: Thursday, February 26, 2026 10:03 PM
To: Olivia Montrose <omontrose@londonlightning.co.uk>
Subject: RE: Tomorrow

Liv,

Why are you emailing me when you are right next to me?
You know, you could just ask me.

Thanks,
Stanley Easton III
Head Coach - London Lightning

From: Olivia Montrose <omontrose@londonlight-
ning.co.uk>
Sent: Thursday, February 26, 2026 10:04 PM
To: Stanley Easton III <seaston@londonlightning.co.uk>
Subject: Tomorrow

Because this is more fun ;)

From: Stanley Easton III <seaston@londonlight-
ning.co.uk>
Sent: Thursday, February 26, 2026 10:04 PM
To: Olivia Montrose <omontrose@londonlightning.co.uk>
Subject: RE: Tomorrow

More fun? Really? I don't think I did a good job of
pleasing you if you're pulling your phone out right now.

Thanks,
Stanley Easton III
Head Coach - London Lightning

From: Olivia Montrose <omontrose@londonlight-
ning.co.uk>
Sent: Thursday, February 26, 2026 10:05 PM
To: Stanley Easton III <seaston@londonlightning.co.uk>
Subject: Tomorrow

I'm being sentimental, Tag. I like emailing with you.

I have no complaints about how I'm feeling right now.

From: Stanley Easton III <seaston@londonlight-
ning.co.uk>
Sent: Thursday, February 26, 2026 10:05 PM
To: Olivia Montrose <omontrose@londonlightning.co.uk>
Subject: RE: Tomorrow

I like emailing with you too. But I like doing other things
more.

Thanks,
Stanley Easton III
Head Coach - London Lightning

From: Olivia Montrose <omontrose@londonlightning.co.uk>
Sent: Thursday, February 26, 2026 10:06 PM
To: Stanley Easton III <seaston@londonlightning.co.uk>
Subject: Tomorrow

We still have to keep this professional.

From: Stanley Easton III <seaston@londonlightning.co.uk>
Sent: Thursday, February 26, 2026 10:07 PM
To: Olivia Montrose <omontrose@londonlightning.co.uk>
Subject: RE: Tomorrow

You're the one who started it. And way to be professional, Liv. No signature? Really?

Thanks,
Stanley Easton III
Head Coach - London Lightning

From: Olivia Montrose <omontrose@londonlightning.co.uk>
Sent: Thursday, February 26, 2026 10:07 PM
To: Stanley Easton III <seaston@londonlightning.co.uk>
Subject: Tomorrow

I'm too in love to care <3

From: Stanley Easton III <seaston@londonlight-
ning.co.uk>
Sent: Thursday, February 26, 2026 10:08 PM
To: Olivia Montrose <omontrose@londonlightning.co.uk>
Subject: RE: Tomorrow

I guess I'll allow it. Only because I love you too <3

Epilogue

OLIVIA - FIVE YEARS LATER

"**M**orning, birthday girl." I press a kiss to Liv's bare shoulder as she stirs in my arms.

"Morning, Tag," Liv purrs.

It's a lazy summer morning. All I want to do is spend the day in bed with her. It's the only plan I made for today.

"Is there anything you'd like to do today on the big birthday?"

"As long as nothing big happens, I'm fine."

I smile into her shoulder and press another kiss there before rolling her onto her back, staring into her sleepy face. Pillow lines crinkle her gorgeous face.

"Oh? And what big things might be happening today?"

"Tag." She lets out that long-suffering sigh she loves giving me. "We've talked about this. There will be no proposing today."

"I know that. It doesn't mean I can't spoil you in other ways today."

Liv and I have spent a lot of time talking about the future. The kind of plans we want to make.

Together.

The Lightning have won the cup these last two seasons. My future here is solid. My future with Liv? Secure.

She still has hard days to work through, but that's okay. She still sees her therapist, and the hard days are few and far between.

Working on yourself isn't easy, but I love her through every one of them.

The one thing that we discussed at length? Her five-year plan. She still wants parts of it to happen.

Like getting married and having kids.

With me.

"How do you plan on spoiling me?"

Tugging the duvet down, I expose her bare chest. Her nipples are already hard as I suck one into my mouth.

"Tag," she groans.

"This is one way I plan on spoiling you."

Drifting down her stomach, I find her pussy already wet for me. I sink a finger inside of her.

"I only need this."

"Oh no." I suck on the pulse at her neck. "This is just the beginning."

"What else?" She arches off the bed as my hand lazily moves in and out of her.

"Well, after mutual orgasms, I plan on making you breakfast."

"I hope not bacon butties." Her face goes serious. "The last time you tried to make them, you almost burned down the flat."

"It was the pan," I correct.

Cooking here is something I'm still not great at.

"It's a good thing the building manager likes me."

"Who wouldn't?" I press my thumb down on her clit to bring her back to the moment and away from the post-fire argument that led to epic makeup sex.

"Mm. What else do you plan on taking me to do today?"

"After breakfast with some champagne, I plan on taking you to all my favorite places in the city."

"Why yours?" she purrs.

"They're your favorites too." I take another nipple in my mouth, laving my tongue around the tight bud.

"Like the Tower Bridge."

"Precisely." I blow my breath over her nipple. "Even if it will be a completely normal, non-private day."

"We can't always do naughty things around the city."

I push two fingers inside her. "Doesn't hurt to try."

Cupping my cheeks, Liv takes my mouth in a heated kiss. Our breaths mingle as I keep working her over. I press my hard dick into her hip as she grinds down onto my hand.

"What else?" she breathes.

"After that, we'll meet everyone for lunch."

"You planned a meal with my friends?"

"Of course. And after that, I plan on bringing you back here and fucking you into oblivion."

"You know, I have a present that you might like too."

"It's your birthday. Why are you getting me a gift?"

"I think a sex toy is a gift for both of us."

"Fuck," I growl.

I move my hand faster, wanting her to come.

It's one of the many reasons I love this woman. She says she's not adventurous, but damn if she doesn't love trying new things in the bedroom.

"I knew you'd like it."

"Then why don't you come for me so we can get this birthday started?"

I nip and suck at her neck. Slide my fingers in and out of her as her hand closes around my cock.

"Yes, baby. Do it. Make me come while you come on my fingers."

"Tag!" Liv shouts, coming unglued. "Yes!"

We both come together. Heat races through me as I pump into her tight fist. "So fucking good, baby."

Lying together, we come down from our high, wrapped up around one another. Just the way I like it.

"You know, you could plan something for next year."

"Already thinking ahead?" I ask, pressing a kiss to her head.

"Yes. Maybe next year we can talk about a proposal."

I smile at her. "Plan on it."

Bonus Epilogue

TAG - ELEVEN MONTHS LATER

Pampering. Check.

Drinks with the girls. Check.

Bridge climb. Check.

Dinner. Check.

Room reservation. Check.

Everything is planned down to the minute. Considering Liv doesn't have a clue, she would be proud of my skills.

I want this day to be a complete surprise to Liv. If I did this on her birthday, she'd know it was coming. But drinks and a day at the spa with the girls? They were all in on helping with the surprise.

The guys? Well, they're helping me get my part ready.

Trying, anyway.

"You were supposed to bring the tape!" Alfie yells, not for the first time. "Stop blaming me that we can't hang this up."

"You said you'd bring the tape. I can show you the text," Jack grumbles.

"Guys. It's fine. We can just throw flower petals over the walkway. It'll be fine."

"It won't look as good without the lights hanging up."

My eyes flit to the city beyond. Dusk has already settled. City lights are popping on all around us. "It'll be fine."

"If she says no, you can blame Jack," Alfie says.

Jack gives him the finger before ripping rose petals off the stalks and throwing them around the table.

All those years ago, I thought I was being so sly renting out the bridge for me and Liv. Turns out, anyone can do this.

What better way to propose to Liv than at our favorite place in the city?

Dinner was delivered earlier. Nothing fancy—sandwiches, so I wouldn't have to worry about it going cold.

Looking at the time, I cut the bickering of the two guys with me. "They should be here soon, so time to cut out."

Stopping, they look around at their work.

It's nothing over-the-top. I wanted to keep it simple.

Some flowers. Champagne. Drinks. No lights, but that's okay.

Honestly, I could have done it all myself, but having to carry this up to the top?

I wanted the help. And the distraction.

"Looks good, mate. I'm sure she'll say yes." Alfie claps me on the shoulder.

"Yeah, and if she doesn't, we'll get pissed after," Jack confirms.

I roll my eyes at them and send them off in the other direction. "Wasn't actually worried, but thanks. Assholes."

River cruises are drifting along under the bridge as I try to wait for Liv. I love her friends, but when I told them what time to be here, I purposefully gave them an earlier time so they might actually be *on time.*

And that time? It's already come and gone. Leaving me to my thoughts.

More and more over the past year, Liv and I have talked about this. Getting married.

Liv didn't want to make a big fuss over the wedding. I can't blame her, but proposing to her? I want to shower her in all the love she shows me every day.

"I want to see why you like this so much," I hear Imogen say.

"Imogen. You've been here before. Why the need to do this?"

The way Liv says Imogen's name brings a smile to my lips. I love how exasperated she gets. Even when it's at me.

Fuck. Now that she's here, the nerves are starting to come.

"Why don't you go first?"

The sound of shoes hitting the top step greets me, and I straighten my shirt.

Liv's favorite gray one with the sleeves rolled up— because I know it drives her crazy.

"Me? What in the world is going on?"

"Bye!"

Liv stumbles into the walkway and damn, does she take my breath away. In a simple black dress that teases her curves, she looks amazing and I drink my fill.

"Sienna! Imogen!" she shouts after them, but when she turns, her eyes go wide. "Tag. What is going on?"

"Hey, baby."

"Umm, hi."

"You look so sexy." I walk toward her, pulling her in and getting a whiff of her perfume. Even after all these years together, the flowery scent still brings me back to that first night.

"What are we doing here? And why do you look so nice?"

"Always with the questions, Liv."

She smiles at me before pressing onto her toes and giving me a sweet kiss. "Well, when I'm shoved up here without any idea of what is going on, I might have one or two."

Grabbing her hand, I lead her down the walkway. The sky is an inky blue now. Lights shimmer off the water. It's just the two of us up here.

The way I like it.

"I thought an early birthday surprise might be in order."

"A surprise?" I can see her mind working, trying to figure out why we're here. I know the second it does because her eyes grow wide and she looks stunned. "Tag, are you…are you doing what I think you're doing?"

Giving her another kiss, I drop down onto one knee. "Yes."

"Oh my God." Her hand flies to cover her mouth as I hold tight to her other one. "I didn't think you'd propose until my birthday."

"Surprise." I beam up at her. "Now—"

"I am definitely surprised," she interrupts. "I didn't think this is what I'd be doing today."

"Well, if I could ask the question, I can confirm this *is* what we're doing today."

"Oh, right." She gives me a sheepish smile. "Go on."

I take a deep breath and start the speech I've had memorized for weeks. "Olivia, I love you. I think I have loved you since the minute I met you and you said hello to me. You are kind and loving. You are generous to a fault and never hesitate to put those you care about before you.

I consider myself the luckiest man in the world to be yours. I never expected to meet you, and somehow, you choose me every day. And if you let me, I will spend my life choosing you. Loving you. Showing you how much you mean to me."

Reaching into my pocket, I pull out the velvet box. I snap it open, and Liv gasps.

"Oh, Tag. It's beautiful."

A Cadenza-style ring with a center diamond surrounded by smaller diamonds on a rose gold band. Unique, just like my Liv.

"Will you marry me, Olivia?"

"Yes!" she shouts, tackling me to the ground. "Yes, yes, yes!"

"Hell, yeah!"

Liv peppers my face with kisses, but grasping her cheeks, I pull her away. First the ring, then the kisses.

Popping it out of its box, I slide the ring down her finger. A perfect fit.

"I love it, Tag. It's stunning."

"Not as stunning as you."

Sliding a hand through her neat hair, I pull the pins out and let it fall around us. I capture her mouth in a slow kiss.

Knowing we're the only ones up here, I take my time with her. I slip my tongue into her mouth. Her fingers hold on tight to me as I savor this moment.

Olivia is it for me. The only person in the world I want to grow old with. I want to make her laugh, make her smile, and even exasperate her.

I want it all.

"I love you so much, baby."

"Not nearly as much as I love you."

"Well, I've got a hotel reservation for us tonight, so we

might have to bet on something to see who loves the other more."

Liv beams down at me.

"Plan on it."

Acknowledgments

BOOK TWENTY-SEVEN IS OUT IN THE WORLD!

I love how all of my stories come together, but this one might be the best! While at RARE Edinburgh, I wanted to do something fun for RARE London. It was my first international signing, so it had to be special. So why not write an entire book?! So over a few too many cocktails, my fabulous PA, Tina, and I, talked through the plot of this book while on a rooftop bar overlooking the city. I had a stack of sticky notes and had to buy a notebook at the airport while in Edinburgh to furiously write down all my ideas! Isn't this the best start to any book?! I still have the early sketch of the special edition just for RARE that I did!

I'll keep this one short and sweet…thank you to all the amazing readers at RARE for being so kind and supportive through the years. You are truly the best part of getting to write books! Who knows…maybe Imogen and Sienna are going to get books at the next RARE London…

Happy reading!
<3 Emily

Sideline Infraction

Illegal Contact

The Big Game

Moose Falls, Maine

Merry in Moose Falls

A Grump in Moose Falls - coming November 7, 2025

Standalones

Off the Deep End

The Highland Escape

Power Pose

Love Pucked - a sapphic hockey romance, coming October 10, 2025

The Ainsworth Royals

Royal Reckoning

Reckless Royal

Royal Relations

Royal Roots

The Love Abroad Series

An Icy Infatuation

A French Fling

A Sydney Surprise

Scan the QR code to read my books now!

About the Author

Image by Tricia B @TheSmutFairy

After winning a Young Author's Award in second grade, Emily Silver was destined to be a writer. She loves writing inclusive stories, with strong heroines and the swoony men who fall for them.

A lover of all things romance, Emily started writing books set in her favorite places around the world. As an avid traveler, she's been to all seven continents and sailed around the globe.

When she's not writing, Emily can be found sipping cocktails on her porch, reading all the romance she can get her hands on and planning her next big adventure!

Find her on social media to stay up to date on all her adventures and upcoming releases!